HARLEY BELL—MONSTER CAMPER

Harley Bell dropped a slice of salami on the floor.

"Pick it up," I said.

"You're not even a regular counselor, you're on trial," said Harley. "Pick it up yourself."

"I'll get it," said Miles. He was the smallest in the group, a thin boy with a serious expression. We watched him pick up the salami, carry it to a garbage pail, and carefully drop it in.

"You little shrimp," Harley sneered. He turned on Douglas. "Hey, whale belly. Want the rest of my sandwich?" Harley threw his sandwich at Douglas. It landed on his lap. The brown mustard smeared on his pants. "Look, the fat slob did it in his pants."

Tears rolled down Douglas' bloated cheeks.

"Hey, hippo," said Harley, "I'm going to do you a favor. I'm going to melt off some of that blubber." He pulled out a wooden kitchen match and whipped it across the tabletop. It exploded into flame. "Okay, blob, your troubles are over."

"Put that out," I roared.

"Make me," said Harley.

Other books by Robert Lipsyte

Robert Lipsyte
SUMMER RULES

An Ursula Nordstrom Book

HarperKeypoint
An Imprint of HarperCollins*Publishers*

Summer Rules
Copyright © 1981 by Robert M. Lipsyte
All rights reserved. No part of this book may be used or reproduced in any
manner whatsoever without written permission except in the case of brief
quotations embodied in critical articles and reviews. Printed in the United
States of America. For information address HarperCollins Children's
Books, a division of HarperCollins Publishers, 10 East 53rd Street, New
York, NY 10022.

Library of Congress Cataloging in Publication Data
Lipsyte, Robert.
    Summer rules.

    SUMMARY: A teen-age boy has to deal with an
unwanted summer camp job, his first love, and some
crucial decisions.
    [1. Camp counselors—Fiction.   2. Camping—
Fiction]   I. Title.
PZ7.L67Su   1981   [Fic]   79-2816
ISBN 0-06-023897-6
ISBN 0-06-023898-4 (lib. bdg.)
ISBN 0-06-447071-7 (pbk.)

Harper Keypoint is an imprint of Harper Trophy, a division of
HarperCollins Publishers. First Harper Keypoint edition, 1992.

For Marjorie

SUMMER RULES

1

I never wanted to work at Happy Valley Day Camp. Better believe it. Taking care of spoiled brats was no real man's job, nothing like the job I had lined up for that summer, my sixteenth, the summer I had been waiting for all my life.

I was going to work on a landscape gardening crew with rough guys who drag raced and hunted and had girl friends who went all the way. I was going to get into great physical shape and have the kind of exciting adventures I needed to become a writer like Ernest Hemingway.

Then my father dumped me back into the playpen with all the other soft city kids and their sissy country summers.

"I hear," he said at dinner, "there's an opening at Happy Valley."

"Better close it quick," I cracked, "before all that happiness spills out."

My father smiled. That should have set off my alarms. My father hated my puns and wisecracks, even when they were funny. But I missed the warning signal because I was daydreaming about getting as strong as a rock and as tanned as leather, and stripping off my shirt for the girls. I didn't even notice how my sister, Michelle, ducked out of the conversation by lowering her head nearly into the chilled purple fruit soup, which she hated.

Usually, Michelle, who was nineteen, would try to top me with some snotty college line like, "That was two thirds of a pun: P.U.," but she didn't say a word. Something big was up, but I was so busy imagining myself on Make-Out Island in the middle of Rumson Lake that I didn't notice a thing.

"An opening for a counselor," continued my father, one of the world's great one-track conversationalists. "I think you'll get it."

"I don't want it," I said.

"Yes, you do," he said.

2

"What makes you think I'm going to apply for it?"

"You already have," he said.

"Marty," said my mother to my father, "you know how I hate cat-and-mouse tactics. Will you please tell Bobby what we've decided."

Finally, my alarms went off. I glanced around the table. No one would look at me. Michelle was trying to drown herself in fruit soup and my mother was staring at my father and he was smiling at his spoon as he paddled it gently through the purple pond. Ripples spread and crashed against the sides of his bowl. A soup storm. How could I have missed all the signals? My father never played with food, even food he hated as much as fruit soup. My mother had made it just for me. She was preparing me for bad news.

"Let's have it," I said. "What's up?"

"Don't you use that tone of voice to your father," said my mother.

"That's just what I mean, Lenore. That tone of voice is part and parcel of his problem."

"What problem?" I asked.

My father looked at me. "The way you carry

3

on. The way you stamp around. The cocky way you seem to have an answer for everything."

Very deliberately, he lifted the spoon out of the soup, shook off a few purple drops, and pointed at me. "You are going to work at Happy Valley this summer."

"I already have a job."

"I don't consider carrying water for the Rumson gang a job."

"It's better than spending the summer wiping the . . ."

"Don't use language like that in front of your mother," said my father.

". . . noses—what did you think I was going to say?—of a bunch of . . ."

"Eat your soup," said my mother, "before it gets warm."

Tears burned my eyes and my nose felt stuffed and something the size of a walnut was stuck in my throat. I had a lot I wanted to say, but all I could get out was, "Why?"

"Someday you'll understand," said my mother. "Eat now, you'll feel better."

"I'll explain it to him now," said my father. I got the feeling he was enjoying this. "The Smiths

4

and the Rumsons and their cousins and their friends are not the type of characters we want you spending your summer with. Every time you turn around one of them is in jail or in the hospital or having to get married.''

It was true. Some of them were pretty wild. Two summers ago, when I was very fat, a bunch of punks led by Willie Rumson gave me a hard time and tried to scare me off my job cutting Dr. Kahn's lawn. But that was then, and this was now. I choked down the walnut and said, ''What's all this got to do with me?''

''Simple. We didn't bring you up to hang around with Rumsons and Smiths.''

''What did you bring me up for, to be one of those phonies and snobs at Happy Valley?''

''Creep!'' snarled Michelle.

''Did you set this up?'' I yelled at her.

''You think I want you at my camp?'' she yelled back. Her eyes were red rimmed.

''Children!'' snapped my mother.

My father leaned back and waggled the spoon. ''None of those Smith and Rumson boys has ever done anything constructive with his life.''

''That makes them bad people to you,'' I said.

"You seem to have a very short memory, Robert," said my father. "It was less than two years ago that Willie Rumson tried to shoot you . . ."

"He didn't even have a slug in the chamber," I said.

". . . and less than one year ago that he set fire to Dr. Kahn's house."

"Only the toolshed. And Willie was the one who called the fire department."

"I can't believe you're defending Willie Rumson," said my mother.

"What's fair is fair," I said. "Besides, he's in jail now for setting that fire. He's paying his debt to society."

"We're getting off the topic," said my father. "Do you understand what I've been trying to say?"

"Sure. The Smiths and the Rumsons aren't good enough for your precious little Bobby."

"You got it," said my father. He put down the spoon. "Case closed."

"No, it's not," I said. "This is a free country. America is still a democracy."

"But this family is not a democracy," said my

father. "It's a dictatorship. And you will do what I tell you until you're on your own, buying your own food and your own clothes and living in your own home."

"Marty," said my mother, patting the air in front of her as if she was soothing an invisible mad dog.

"No, I think we better get something straight, once and for all." Grape-sized muscles were popping along his jaw. "I'm getting fed up with your attitude. Big shot. Know-it-all. Wise guy."

"Flattery will get you nowhere."

"See what I mean?" he shouted. "You talk back to me like that and yet you still expect me to teach you to drive this summer?"

That stopped me like a punch in the nose. The day I'd turned sixteen I had taken out a Learner's Permit. As soon as I passed my driving test I would get a Junior License, which meant I could drive alone in the daytime and with a regular licensed driver next to me at night. It wasn't as good as full-time wheels, but it was a start.

"I'm sorry," I said.

"He's just saying that," said Michelle.

"Who asked you?"

"Children!"

"Then it's settled," said my father.

I couldn't go down without at least a little fight. "You can't stop me from being friends with Jim Smith, you can't stop me from seeing . . ."

"I won't let you use the car if I think you're going to be with dangerous characters." He turned away. "Lenore, what's for dinner besides this purple mess?"

"Happy Valley," I sneered. "Don't be sure those aren't dangerous characters up there."

"What do you mean, Bobby?" asked my mother.

"You know what I mean," I said. "If you spend your time with fruits and nuts, you could get to be one, too."

2

Happy Valley. What a laugh. They should have called it Pathetic Molehill.

The Happy Valley Bungalow Colony was a collection of small, dirty-white, ramshackle cottages, some without indoor toilets or kitchens, bunched together on a little hill on the other side of Rumson Lake from our house. The Bell family, who owned Happy Valley, rented the bungalows for the summer to people from the city. They also ran a day camp that was open to kids from six to thirteen years old, whether or not they lived in the colony. There was bus service for counselors and campers who lived off the grounds, as we did. The camp consisted of a swimming area on Rumson Lake, a shack for arts and crafts, a handball wall, and a scrubby softball field at the foot of a meadow that needed mowing. A crummy-looking place. I never could understand why it meant so much to Michelle. This was going to be her third summer in a row as a counselor at Happy Valley. The thought of my working at her camp was driving her crazy.

She started complaining again the minute she backed my parents' black Dodge out of the driveway and eased it down the hill toward the county road. We were going to the first counselors' meeting of the season.

"This is going to be some great summer," she muttered, "let me tell you."

"So tell me about it, sweetheart," I said, just like Humphrey Bogart. Bogie and Alan Ladd, especially in *Shane*, were my favorite actors. I even took a deep drag on an imaginary cigarette and blew the smoke into her eyes.

"Will you stop that! It's corny, it's juvenile, and it's not even a good imitation."

"Whatsa matter, kiddo? You afraid I'm gonna put a crimp in your sex life?"

That must have gotten to her, because she shut up. Her teeth snapped together. I turned on the radio and when she had nothing to say about that, I tuned in a station playing rock and roll. Even when "Shake, Rattle, and Roll" came on, she kept quiet. Michelle hated that song. I wasn't crazy about it myself, but the way I was feeling, anything that bothered Michelle couldn't be all bad. My father and mother must have put pressure on her to get me the job at Happy Valley, but she'd done it, hadn't she? She was on their side.

The county road curved around Rumson Lake. This morning, the sun reflected off the tips of little waves kicked up by a gentle breeze. The lake looked beautiful and I loved Rumson Lake, but every diamond sparkling on the water might just as well have been a cold pebble in my mouth.

Hey, that's not a bad line, I thought. I dug my pencil and notebook out of the back pocket of my chino pants and wrote it down: *Every diamond sparkling on the water might just as well have been a cold pebble in my mouth now that Pedro was dead and the girl was in the clutches of the bandits.*

A writer has to get his good lines down or he'll forget them. That's why I didn't go any-

11

where without a little spiral-bound notebook and one of those stubby pencils you use to keep score in miniature golf.

"Little Ernest Hemingway," sneered Michelle.

"Obscenity," I replied. Hemingway never used dirty words in his books, just the word "obscenity," like "You're an obscenity" or "You're full of obscenity." If it was good enough for Papa Hemingway, it was good enough for me.

"When are you going to stop acting like a baby?" asked Michelle. She turned off the county road and started up the narrow blacktop that led to Happy Valley. "Moe Bell thinks you're eighteen years old. If he finds out you're sixteen, he'll fire you."

"Okay by me."

"And Dad'll *never* let you use the car."

I wasn't going to roll over and play dead for her just because she was right. "If he finds out about me, he'll find out you've been lying to him for the last three years."

"You know something, Bobby, I'm beginning to think Dad was right. You're a wise guy. An answer for everything. You used to be nice."

"Sure," I said. "When I was just a fat kid everyone could feel sorry for. Or pick on."

She snorted. "And now that you're God's gift to the world, you've got a right to be nasty."

"You got it, sweeetheart," I Bogied. "I'm making up for all that lost time."

That ended the conversation, but what good did it do me? No matter what I said, my fate was sealed. Death Valley Day Camp.

At the top of the hill, Michelle turned off the blacktop onto an unpaved dirt road that separated the cottages and the general store from the day camp and the casino, a huge old renovated barn. The casino was the social center of the bungalow colony. At night and on weekends it was used for dances and parties and bingo and movies. During the week, when day camp was in session, it was used for indoor activities, and lunch and rest hour for the campers. On the roof of the casino was painted the Bell family emblem, the outline of a bell with a smiling face inside. Talk about corny.

Michelle drove onto a grassy area under some trees near the casino. A dozen cars were already parked there.

"We're late, hurry up," she said. She checked her face in the rearview mirror. After she saw it was still there she jumped out of the car.

I followed her to the casino's sagging wooden front porch. A little redheaded boy, nine or ten years old, was stretched out across the steps, blocking our way.

"Excuse us, Harley," said Michelle.

"A nickel to get through," said the kid. "I'm a tollbooth."

His hair was fire-engine red. He had bright blue eyes and a snub nose and a million freckles. He looked like a model for all those *Saturday Evening Post* covers of snubnosed freckle-faced redheaded kids. Until you looked real close. He had a mean expression on his little face.

"We're late, Harley," said Michelle in one of her phony sweet voices, "and Moe will be so mad if . . ."

"Tough titty."

I said to the kid, "Listen, Red, move on over before I move on over you."

"Oh, no," whispered Michelle, "you have to treat him with understanding." She studied psychology at Barnard College. "Harley, please don't make us have to step over you."

"You try it and I'll kick you where the sun don't shine. Now the price is a nickel each."

"Give it to him," said Michelle. "I have no change."

"I'll give him a rap in the . . ."

"Just a nickel, Bobby."

"Why are you giving in to this . . ."

"Because we're late and Moe Bell hates lateness and if you get fired Dad won't let you . . ."

"Okay." I gave the kid a nickel.

"I said a nickel each."

"That's all you get, pal." I made my voice an icicle.

Michelle sighed. "Bobby Marks, meet Harley . . . Bell."

"Bell." I gave him the second nickel.

Harley jumped up, said, "Up yours," and ran away. He moved like a jackrabbit.

"Do we have to pay off that little obscenity every time we want to go in here?"

"He looks so cute," said Michelle, "and he's got such deep-seated problems."

"Problems? He's a juvenile delinquent. What

15

do they teach you in Psych, that Hitler had problems?''

''You've got problems,'' said Michelle, ''and you're not even cute.''

We walked into the casino. It took a few seconds for my eyes to adjust to the dimness of the huge, stuffy, dingy old barn. At least a dozen college-age guys and girls were sitting on folding wooden chairs at the far end of the casino, in front of the stage. On the stage, Moe Bell, a big, bald, energetic man in blue Bermuda shorts and a Happy Valley Day Camp tee-shirt was waving his long, hairy arms and yelling, ''More in 'fifty-four. Let's hear it, counselors. More in 'fifty-four.''

Michelle marched right up to the front row of folding chairs and sat down. I followed her because I didn't want to sit alone and I didn't know anyone else, but I felt naked up there. I hate to sit in the front row of anywhere. Writers should sit in the back, or off to one side, so they can observe the entire scene. But that's not the reason I hate to sit in the front row. People who think they look like Michelle thinks she looks are always sitting in the front so they can be seen

16

and admired. It's not that I'm ugly or a freak or anything, but until I was fourteen years old I was very fat and sometimes I still think I am. I'm always a little surprised to pass a mirror and see the reflection of a normal-sized person.

Moe Bell looked directly down at me. "Bobby Marks, the newest addition to our staff. Better late than never. What do you say, Bobby?"

I felt like a fool, but I blurted, "More in 'fifty-four?"

"That's the spirit." Moe beamed. "More in 'fifty-four means that the summer of 1954 is going to be a Super-Duper Extra-Special Yankee Doodle Ipsy-Dipsy A-Number-One True-Blue Hot-Diggety Bell-Ringing Wing-Ding for all the folks at Happy Valley. So let's hear it loud and proud. MORE IN 'FIFTY-FOUR!"

Everybody started yelling, "MORE IN 'FIFTY-FOUR," even Dr. Michelle Freud. So I did, too. It was dumb, but it felt good.

"Love ya," shouted Moe. There was sweat on top of his shiny bald head, and the smiling bell on his tee-shirt swayed. Michelle said he could be a real pain to work for sometimes, but that he was the best of the Bells. His older brother, Irving, who owned the bungalow colony, and his sister, Rose, who was in charge of the general store, were famous for being cheap and nasty. During the winter, Moe was an assistant principal in a junior high school in the city.

"Okay, counselors. Now we'll hear from some members of our senior staff. Batting number one, our director of athletics, the man with muscles in places most of us don't even have places . . . Al Rapp."

"YO," came a shout from the back of the casino, and then the *slap-slap-slap-slap* of high-top white basketball sneakers running along the wooden floor.

Whomp. Al Rapp leaped to the stage in a single bound. Everybody applauded, even Michelle. He made a quick little bow and waved away the applause, as if to say Nothing to it, folks.

He was wearing only gym trunks. I guess he didn't want to deprive us of too much of his powerhouse body. Above the neck he was ordinary looking. He had a wilted blond crew cut and weak brown eyes that blinked nervously behind horn-rimmed glasses. I figured he was about twenty and didn't have to shave too often.

"There's big news in 'fifty-four," said Al. His voice was ordinary, too. "For the first time in Happy Valley history, we'll be playing in the Inter-Camp League. We'll be playing against Laughing Rock and Wishing Well and Lenape and our traditional rivals . . . Mohawk Hill!"

As he talked, he flexed his muscles. Like punctuation. A softball-sized bicep jumped in the middle of a sentence, his tree-trunk chest bulged at the end. I wondered if he had figured it all out in front of a full-length mirror, which muscles were commas and which were periods.

"We're going to get out there and kick their cans, leave 'em in the dust, show 'em what we're made of."

"You're made of pure crap," muttered a voice a few rows back. It wasn't loud enough to carry up to Moe and Al on stage.

I twisted around until I located the voice. It came from a small, sharp face surrounded by a thicket of black curls. Green eyes blazed at me. I turned away fast, my face suddenly hot.

"We're with ya all the way, Allie baby," shouted Moe. He led the applause for Al Rapp.

"And now, a man who needs no introduction, our own star . . . Jerry Silver!"

Jerry Silver glided over the floor and up the little flight of steps to the stage. He was tall and slender, with a lion's mane of brown hair, which he tossed when he got to the center of the stage. According to Michelle, who had talked about him a lot last summer, he was about twenty-one. He was studying music and dramatics in college. Naturally, he was the music and dramatics counselor.

He took a deep drag on a cigarette and let the smoke curl out of his mouth and up into his nose. Then he swallowed and blew out a perfect ring. I had never seen such fancy smoking.

"The hot news in 'fifty-four from Silverstar Productions is this: We're doing *The King and I* this year and for the first time in Happy Valley history, counselors will perform the major roles." He blew another smoke ring while the hot news sank in.

"Guess who's going to play the king," muttered that voice with the black curls and the green eyes.

Jerry Silver had more to say and there were

other speeches after that, but I barely heard them. The waterfront counselor talked about water safety and the arts and crafts counselor talked about wallets and lanyards and the counselor in charge of transportation read the schedule of bus duty, but I kept twisting around for a better look at that green-eyed girl. I didn't get a better look and she didn't make any more wisecracks.

When the meeting was over, Al Rapp slap-slapped up to Michelle. "You're looking great, Michelle." He was shorter than he had appeared to be on stage, shorter than I. He was about Michelle's height.

"How have you been, Allan?" asked Michelle in that slightly bored voice she majored in at college. "I think some of your muscles seem to have grown muscles since last summer."

Al found something fascinating to study on the floor between his sneakers. "Oh, I've been working out." He was quivering with joy. Michelle has that effect on some guys.

"This is my brother, Bobby. He's going to be working here this summer."

"Glad to have you aboard," said Al. He hadn't caught the disgust in Michelle's voice. He stuck out his hand at me. "So you're the famous ex-blimp I heard so much about."

That's not exactly what I wanted to be famous for, but I was flattered that Michelle had talked about me, so I just grinned and nodded. I shook his hand. It felt like a leather bag filled with iron bolts.

Jerry Silver appeared. He kissed Michelle on the cheek. "Lovelier than ever, m'dear."

He offered me a hand as damp and limp as a fish. "Brother Roberto, welcome. Join us at Happy Valley as we slide over the razor blade of life."

I winced—I couldn't help myself. Michelle smiled. She loves that pseudointellectual crud, she really eats it up, especially from older guys.

"What do you think of *The King and I*?" asked Jerry.

"Sooo original," said Michelle. That's her style of flirting, acting bored and being sarcastic.

Jerry took his time fishing a pack of Pall Malls out of the pocket of his white tennis shirt. He shook out a cigarette. "I've already decided who simply *must* play Anna." He pointed the unlit cigarette at Michelle.

Michelle tried very hard to look bored, but she didn't make it. "I've never sung on stage."

"Leave it to me, I'll make you a star." Jerry tossed his head. His lion's mane flew up and settled back into place. I wondered how he got his hair to behave like that. "Or maybe, my sweet, I'll just make you."

"That'll be the day," snickered Al.

"Why don't you go somewhere and lift a dumbbell," said Jerry sharply. "Or talk to one."

Al raised his right hand like a meat cleaver. "You know, Jerry, if my hands weren't registered as lethal weapons I'd break open your head like a ripe watermelon."

"Those are actually your hands?" asked Jerry, popping his eyes. "All these years I thought you were wearing mittens."

Michelle clapped, loud, lazy claps with at least a whole second between each one, the snottiest claps I had ever heard.

"You ought to take your act on the Ed Sullivan show," she said. She had fully recovered her bored and sarcastic voice.

"By the by," said Jerry. "You're all invited to

23

Silverstar's third annual Cocktail Party and Mixed Doubles in the Bushes. Next Saturday.''

I thought of the green-eyed girl and looked around, but she wasn't in the casino anymore. Most of the other counselors had already left. I thought she might be outside. I said good-bye to Al and Jerry, and told Michelle I'd meet her at the car. Moe Bell ambushed me on the way to the door.

''Bobby, I was so disappointed that you came late to the first meeting.'' His round face looked sad.

What could I say? I would have been early if Michelle hadn't spent so much time in the bathroom making herself look as if she didn't care how she looked. I said, ''It won't happen again.''

''That's good, because I like you, I really do.'' He bobbed his head a few times. ''That's why I took a chance on you, a counselor with no experience whatsoever, only eighteen years old. I saw something in you and I hope you won't ever disappoint me again.''

''I'll try not to,'' I mumbled, very uncomfortable because he kept his face so close to mine as we talked that I could feel his hot breath every time he said a word with *b* or *p* or *t* in it.

"Now, I want to talk to you about your assignment. When I hired you, I said you'd probably be in charge of a group of nine- and ten-year-old boys, but at the last minute the young man who had that group last summer returned to us." Moe Bell smiled, as if that should make me as happy as it made him. "So, naturally, I gave him his old group back. Wouldn't you have done the same thing?"

"I guess so."

"Well, since I don't have a group for you, you'll be what we call a utility counselor. Your assignment will vary from day to day, you'll do whatever needs to be done. Sounds interesting, doesn't it?" He nodded his head before I could answer. "Of course, there's a little problem."

"Money?"

"You really are a quick mind, Bobby. If you're not a regular counselor, I can't very well give you a regular counselor's salary, can I? It wouldn't be fair to the regular counselors." He shook his head.

"How much?" I croaked. The old walnut was back in my throat.

"A utility counselor gets half as much as a regular beginning counselor, so . . ." He spread out his long, hairy arms and smiled.

"Seventy-five dollars? For the whole summer?"

"Of course, if you don't want the job . . ." He put on his sad face again.

"Okay." I turned away just in case the burning I felt in my eyes spilled out in tears. I really hated it when someone took advantage of me and there was nothing I could do about it.

"Bobby? You're leaving without a good-bye?" Moe sounded disappointed in me already. Michelle was right, he was a pain.

I turned and said, "Good-bye."

"Till Monday," he said. "Oh, we're going to have a great summer. Such fun. You remember our slogan?"

"More in 'fifty-four." I loaded as much sarcasm as I could into every word, but it was a waste. Moe Bell just smiled and patted me on the shoulder.

"Believe me, Bobby, it's going to be a humdinger."

3

"How much they paying you?" asked Jim Smith. He rolled a toothpick with his tongue across his lower lip and into a corner of his mouth.

"A beginning regular counselor gets about a hundred and fifty dollars for the summer plus tips," I said. It wasn't an outright lie and I was ashamed to tell him the truth.

"You'da made more'n twice as much with us."

"Yeah, I know."

"Your business." He shrugged and turned his back on me and bent down to study the engine of his Chevy. Through the back of his oily blue tee-shirt I could see the outlines of his shoulder blades and his ribs. Jim Smith was the best of the Rumsons. He was Willie's cousin. Two summers ago, when Willie was on my back, Jim saved me a couple of times; but he did it mostly out of loyalty to Willie, to keep him from getting into really big trouble. Last summer, though, Jim and I started to become friends. We were clearing some land behind Dr. Kahn's house, and we found out we both loved cowboy movies. Tuesday night was Western Night at the Rumson Lake Theater, and sometimes we'd run into each other in town, and talk about the flick for an hour on the streetcorner. Two of our favorites were *The Return of the Durango Kid* and *Lash LaRue Rides Again!*

I knew that after a while Jim would lift his head out of the engine and continue the conversation, so I just found a nearby fender to lean on and gazed around the junkyard behind Lester Smith's Auto Body Repair as if a part I needed was somewhere in one of those twisted, rusted clumps of dead Fords and Studebakers and Chevys.

Most of those cars had just gotten old and given out. I knew that, but I wondered how many of them had died suddenly, smashing into a tree at ninety miles an hour or colliding head-on with a farmer's truck while trying to pass on a double-line curve on the road between Rumson Lake and Lenape Falls.

There were always little stories in the *Rumson Lake Gazette* about this Rumson or that Smith recuperating in Grantsville Hospital after a crash. The Smiths and the Rumsons weren't the only families who lived all year around in Rumson Lake Township, but there seemed to be more of them than anybody else, and they seemed to get into more trouble—my father was right about that. But they also had more members on the village council, and the police sergeant was a Smith, and a lot of the plumbers and electricians and builders and storekeepers were Smiths or Rumsons or married to Smith or Rumson women.

After a while, Jim lifted his head out of the engine and turned around. "Where's your car?"

"I hitched into town."

"Car broke down?"

I nodded. Jim was another one who didn't know exactly how old I was. He wouldn't believe that I didn't even have my *junior* license yet. Of course, Smiths and Rumsons never let little things like licenses get in the way of their driving.

29

In that family, you qualified the day your foot reached the accelerator.

"Want me to look at your car?"

"No, that's all right." I didn't know what to do with my hands so I stuck them in my pockets. "We would have had a great summer."

Jim rolled the toothpick back to the other corner of his mouth, chewed on his gum for a few seconds, then spat into the dirt between his scuffed black boots. Spitting, chewing gum, rolling a toothpick around, even smoking, all at the same time, was a Smith and Rumson trademark. I had practiced just rolling the toothpick around, but I never could get it right. Once I even got splinters in my tongue.

"Look, here, Marks, you don't have to tell me if you don't want to. . . ."

"My parents. My father, mostly. He's making me take the camp job."

"Don't want you associating with us, huh?"

"No, it's not like that, he . . . uh . . . well, he thinks working in camp will look better on my college application."

"Yeah, 'spect it will." He slammed shut the hood and wiped his greasy hands on his dungarees.

"I'm sorry you had to go to all that trouble talking your father into hiring me."

"Forget it. He'd just as lief you didn't work with us. You know what he thinks about summer people. He like to go crazy last night—he was in town and this fat old cow, she must of been fifty years old, she was walking down Main Street in red shorts—red shorts!—and one of those halter tops, her boobs was bouncing right out of them."

"She must have been a renter," I said quickly. "My father can't stand those people, either. It's disgusting the way they dress, the people who just rent for the summer. People who own their own homes are different, they never . . ."

"They're all summer people to my old man," said Jim. "Well . . ." He swung behind the wheel of his Chevy. He started the engine and listened to it with his eyes closed. After a while, he nodded at the sound.

"Guess I'll see you around," I said. I was hoping he'd offer me a ride, but I didn't want to come out and ask him because I didn't want to take the chance he would turn me down. I felt bad enough as it was. The last time we'd talked alone, when he'd told me his father had finally agreed to take me on as a helper for the summer, we'd made a lot of plans. Jim was going to take me around to all the country bars where they never ask for your draft card and he was going to teach me to soup up a car and I was going to introduce him to a lot of summer girls he had only admired from a distance. We would have had a great summer.

"Yeah, see you around." He slammed shut the car door.

Just to keep the conversation going, I said, "You been visiting Willie lately?"

He nodded. "Willie might be coming out soon."

"What?" I felt like my insides had been flushed with icewater.

"He's not going to bother nobody."

"He's going to come after me. He still blames me for everything that happened to him. You told me yourself he still thinks if I had quit Dr. Kahn's like he wanted me to he would have gotten the job and he never would have . . ."

"You don't have to worry about Willie no more. He's changed."

"How?"

Jim shifted the toothpick from side to side. "Some bad things happened to him in jail. They gave him electric shock treatments and injections." He shook his head sorrowfully. "Willie's sweet as pie now."

"That's good."

"Not for Willie. The shocks affected his brain. He's like a zombie." Before I could ask Jim if Willie's zombie condition was permanent, he gunned the engine and leaned out of the window. "Happy Valley, huh?"

"That's right."

"We got some jobs up there, maybe I'll look for you. Take care they don't turn you into a queer."

"What do you mean?"

Jim laughed through his nose. "Some of those guys up there look like they pee sitting down."

He spun out and left me with the taste of burning rubber.

4

As soon as I got off the camp bus that first morning, Moe Bell pulled me aside and pushed his big face to within an inch of mine. "Bobby!" he said, as if he was thrilled to see me. All those *b*'s exploded in my face. They smelled of fried eggs and salami. "Feeling strong?"

He didn't wait for an answer. "That's terrific. Now you remember I told you I was going to give you a chance to prove yourself. Show us you're worth your money. Report to Rose on the double. She's waiting for you at the store."

He gave me a little pat on the can to get me going.

I trotted out of the parking area and across the dirt road that separated the camp and the casino from the bungalow colony and the store. I even put on a little burst of speed to show Moe Bell I was gung ho. But once there were a few trees between us I stopped and turned around. The entire camp was assembling around the flagpole for Opening Day Ceremonies. All the counselors would be introduced, the kids would be divided into their groups, there would be jokes and speeches and songs. Everyone would get to know each other. I began to feel bad about being left out. Then I remembered that I never wanted to be here in the first place.

Rose Bell was waiting for me on the steps of the general store. She was small and dark. She looked like a crow. "Let's go, let's go." She sounded like a crow. I expected her to flap her arms.

I followed her inside.

The Happy Valley general store was dimly lit by sunlight filtering through dirt-encrusted windows and a single naked bulb hanging by a black wire from a ceiling beam. I made out shelves loaded with cans and boxes and bags. There was a dusty counter, with an old cash register at one end and some open jars of penny candy on the other. Flies darted in and out of the jars. They seemed to prefer peppermint. An old refrigerator in a corner vibrated and sneezed.

"You. Here's a list." Rose Bell handed me a piece of paper. "Bring everything on that list to the kitchen in the casino. Don't take all summer."

It was a long list, mostly of giant economy size cans of purple plums and pears and applesauce and pineapple juice and grapefruit juice.

"How should I bring them over?"

"You got arms, legs? You crippled?" She pecked at me with her little bird eyes.

"Well, what I meant, if I could load them all into a car . . ."

"Car? That's all you kids think about these days, you can't go across the street without getting into a car."

"Just to save time," I said. "It would be more efficient."

"Efficient? What do you know about efficient? You're an expert?" She shook her head and started for the door. "There's a wheelbarrow out back."

There was no order to the shelves. The cans of different fruits and juices were mixed together and some of them were behind bottles of ketchup or under bags of charcoal and boxes of soap flakes. Almost every single can was dented. Most of them had brown stains on their labels and patches of rust on the tin. I piled them all in the middle of the store. I was going to sort them as I carried them out to the wheelbarrow so they could be stacked in order at the casino kitchen. I figured about four wheelbarrow loads would do the job.

"What's this? Everything on the floor?" The crow was back.

"I thought it would be more efficient if . . ."

"What if a customer comes in?" She flapped her arms. "What's your name?"

"Robert Jordan," I said. I tried to swallow it back, but it was out before I had a chance.

Rose Bell flapped out while I was trying to figure out how I could be so dumb. If there's one thing adults hate, it's a smart aleck. It drives them wild. Mom and Dad are always warning me that my big mouth is going to get me into serious trouble someday. Of course, I think it's going to save me from serious trouble, that I'll talk myself out of jams.

I stacked the purple plums and the pears care-

fully on the wheelbarrow. As if they were dynamite. Just the way Robert Jordan would stack the
explosives before he went to blow up the bridge.
I felt better. Rose Bell didn't seem like the kind
of person who remembered people's names anyway. And she certainly didn't seem like she
would know that Robert Jordan was the hero of
For Whom the Bell Tolls, my favorite Hemingway
book, which I had just finished reading for the
third time.

For Whom the Bell Tolls. Now there's a pun.
Too bad there wasn't anyone around to share it
with. I had a friend named Joanie Miller who
really appreciated my sense of humor. She went
to my school in the city and her parents owned a
summer home on Rumson Lake that was within
walking distance of ours. But they went to Europe
this summer for their vacation. Joanie would
have really appreciated my Bell line. I started to
miss her. Then I remembered she was dating
college men these days.

I pushed the loaded wheelbarrow over the
unpaved, rutted road that snaked among the
ramshackle bungalows. The morning sun was
rising above the trees and its warmth felt good

on my back. It was quiet in the bungalow colony. Except for a few babies sleeping in carriages under insect netting, all the children were at the day camp. There were no men around except for a few very old guys rocking away on little porches. The men were in the city, working. They drove up Friday nights to spend the week-ends with their families. The women were hanging out wash or working on their suntans or playing canasta and Mah-Jongg on folding tables set up on the grass in front of the bungalows.

The wheelbarrow was heavy and I had to hunch forward to steer it. I felt good. I didn't mind working hard as long as nobody was looking over my shoulder all the time, checking the lawn for blades of grass I'd missed or the rug for lint I didn't vacuum.

The heat and the quiet and the rutted road and tall trees helped me pretend I was Robert Jordan in the mountains of Spain, fighting the Fascist pigs. The submachine gun was heavy on my shoulder and the grenades rattled in my pocket but I couldn't stop because the guerrillas were waiting for me to lead them through the dark pine forest to that obscenity of a bridge.

When I got to the casino, the campers and counselors were all sitting around the flagpole singing the camp song.

> Far above Lake Rumson's waters,
> On a hill of green,
> Stands a camp called Happy Valley,
> Best we've ever seen.

I felt sorry for them, singing a dippy little song while I was giving my life for democracy. I wheeled my fearful cargo to the kitchen at the back of the casino.

"You can bring those submarines right up here," said the voice with green eyes.

She was framed in the doorway of the casino kitchen, looking down at me. Her eyes were even greener than I remembered, sea green, so dazzlingly green they made me blink.

Her black curls were tucked under a red bandanna. Her skin was smooth and pale. She had a small, sharp nose. She wore bright red lipstick.

The heat I had felt on my back spilled into my stomach, my groin, my legs.

"Submarines?" I croaked.

"Sure. Can't you tell?"

I hated to admit I didn't know what she was talking about so I just shrugged.

"Don't you know what a submarine is?" She had a long knife in one hand and half a salami in the other. She was pointing them both at me.

"Sure, a submarine's a boat that can . . ."

"No." She sounded disgusted. "Come on with those cans. I've got a lot of work to do." She turned her back on me.

Showing off, I carried up four cans at a time and stacked them in a corner of the kitchen. Usually when I show off like that, I drop something, or at least stumble. But not this time. Robert Jordan was as surefooted as a mountain goat and he handled the purple plums as if they were merely dynamite.

"So what are you trying to prove?" she asked over her shoulder. "You trying to rupture yourself?"

I couldn't think of anything to say so I just snuck out.

She didn't bother to turn around when I arrived with the second wheelbarrow load. I cleared my throat and banged a few cans together as I stacked them, but she just kept slicing bread and salami on a long table against one wall of the dim kitchen. The Bells certainly didn't waste their money on electric lights.

Finally, I said, "Okay, I give up. What's a submarine?"

She turned around. "There's a fire in a supermarket and the firemen flood the place with water to put it out. Do you follow me?" She spoke slowly and waved the knife like a teacher with a ruler.

When I nodded, she continued: "Now the supermarket holds a fire sale and all the cans that have been underwater, they're called submarines, are sold cheap to finks who feed them to people who won't know the difference."

"Like kids in day camp," I said brightly.

"Like people in old-age homes and hospitals and insane asylums and day camps." A red spot appeared on each of her pale cheeks. She was angry. She was beautiful.

"Do you think this stuff is bad for you?"

"Who wants to find out?" She turned her back again, dismissing me.

I'm sure I set a record racing back to the store,

reloading the wheelbarrow and rattling over the rutted road to the casino kitchen.

"Back already?" She didn't look overjoyed to see me. "You some kind of a brownnose?"

"No," I replied as coolly as I could with a parched tongue, "I'm just trying to win the Moe Bell Prize."

The green eyes narrowed. "The what?"

"You know, Nobel Prize, Moe Bell Prize."

"That's what I thought you said."

"Just a pun," I apologized, "really only two thirds of a pun: P.U."

She almost smiled. "You're very witty."

I lost my breath.

"Really, that was very witty." She did smile. It was wonderful. "What's your name?"

"Let's go, let's go," cawed Rose Bell, flying into the kitchen. "It's almost lunchtime. You haven't finished the sandwiches." Rose Bell turned on me. "What are you standing around for?"

Both of them were looking at me and I tried to come up with an answer, a smart-aleck answer that would show the girl with the gorgeous green eyes that I wasn't afraid of Rose Bell. But my mind was a blank.

"So go then," ordered Rose Bell, and I slunk out of the kitchen. I looked over my shoulder. The girl was bending over her salami sandwiches and Rose Bell was standing behind her, hands on her hips.

"And you. Is this how you thank us for getting you out of the city this summer? Answer me, Sheila."

I didn't hear her answer but I knew her name. Sheila.

5

"Ten miles an hour," said my father. "You let it creep up to eleven and we go home."

Try keeping a Dodge V-8 with Fluid Drive at ten miles an hour on a stretch of road that's straight as an arrow and deserted. Not another car in sight. Farmland on both sides of the road. All-year-rounders call it Drag Alley.

"If I drove this slow on the county road," I said, "they'd arrest me as a menace to traffic."

"You are learning control," said my father. "When you can stop on a dime and make all your turns at five miles an hour, then we'll consider going a little faster."

"Hot diggety," I said, a little too sarcastically.

"Don't talk yourself out of the driver's seat," warned my father.

I eased my foot off the accelerator. The speedometer needle was quivering at 10, ready to rise.

"But don't drop to nine, either," he said. "Control, Robert, control is the secret word."

Control. Sometimes, when he said it, I wasn't sure if he was talking only about driving, or Life, too. My father could be a hard guy to figure out. But as long as I was behind the wheel, I didn't wrack my brain. My father had taken off work the first two weeks in July, and every afternoon when I got back from camp he gave me a driving lesson.

The first day, we never left the driveway. He only let me start the car and turn it off, and work the lights and the windshield wipers until I could handle every knob and switch on the dashboard without looking. The second day he let me shift gears, in the driveway. On the third day, he drove us to the back roads, and I got to drive five miles an hour, forward and reverse, stop and start. On the fourth day, I got up to ten miles an hour and I started doing right-hand turns.

Even at ten miles an hour I felt that horsepower surging up my arms and into my brain, where it wasn't hard to imagine tooling along on

my own with a girl by my side. Sheila? After Rose
Bell chased me out of the kitchen that first morning, I hadn't gotten another chance to talk to
Sheila all week. She wasn't around the casino
when I came back with the last wheelbarrow
load, and then Moe Bell assigned me to spread a
few tons of white gravel around the bungalows. I
spent very little time near the day camp, and I
only saw Sheila twice, from a distance. Even
Michelle wasn't sure who she was.

"Easy, easy," said my father, in that strained
voice he used whenever he saw another car
within five miles of me or a ditch he thought was
out to get me. He didn't have a lot of confidence
in my ability to stop a car hurtling along at ten
miles an hour.

"What is it?" I asked.

"Car's coming."

"Where?"

"Both hands on the wheel, please."

"But it's so far away," I said.

"You have to anticipate, you have to think for
the other driver. What if he's drunk, having a
heart attack, what if he's momentarily blinded by

47

the sun? Are you ready to react to the situation, to take control?''

I could only think, What if it's somebody I know seeing me creep along Drag Alley at ten miles an hour with my father poised to grab the wheel?

As the other car approached, I twisted my facial features so they couldn't be recognized and scrunched low in the seat. The other car whizzed past without a heart attack.

''That was good, I liked the way you held the road,'' said my father. ''Tomorrow we'll go on to left-hand turns and parallel parking.''

He told me to stop and we switched seats. My father relaxed once he got behind the wheel. The little muscles along his jaw stopped twitching. We cruised toward home at thirty-five miles per hour, the late afternoon sun reflecting off the black hood of the Dodge and filling the front seat with a golden haze.

''Anything new at Happy Valley?'' he asked.

''Yeah. Moe said he's going to let me start working with a group tomorrow.''

''That sounds like progress to me.''

"I don't know. I was getting used to being by myself. I get ideas for stories."

"Working with a group sounds a lot more interesting than raking gravel," said my father.

"I guess so." It was too warm and cozy in the car to get into an argument.

"Aren't you sorry now you put up such a fuss about going to Happy Valley?" It was a rhetorical question, no answer required.

"Dad? When you were a kid did your parents ever make you do something you didn't want to do?"

"It was such a different time then, money was so tight, there just weren't the same kinds of opportunities for young people. You just can't compare . . ." He smiled. "Well, once, I was a little older than you, a man came around the neighborhood, I remember he was wearing cowboy boots and a ten-gallon hat, in Brooklyn yet, and he was signing up boys to go West and fight fires."

"Forest fires?" I had never heard this story before.

"That's right. It was some kind of government project. We were going to live in bunk-

49

houses and ride horses and fight fires. Your grandmother wouldn't hear of it.''

"How come?''

"She was afraid I wouldn't finish college. I was just starting then, going at night and working days. And I guess she was also worried I'd get hurt, or fall in with dangerous characters. . .''

"Rumsons and Smiths," I said without thinking. But he didn't get angry.

"Something like that.''

"Why didn't you just go anyway?''

He looked at me sharply. "Young people minded their parents in those days.''

"You ever sorry now you didn't go?''

He chewed on his lower lip. Usually, my father didn't take much time to think of answers to my questions—he either snapped out a reply or ignored me. Finally, he said: "I never did get to see the West. It might have been exciting. A real adventure. Risking your life and doing good. Who knows?''

"I'll never hold my son back," I said.

"We'll see, we'll see when the time comes.''

I suddenly noticed that we were driving up the hill to the house. Mom and Michelle would be getting dinner ready, and Dad and I wouldn't have a chance to talk anymore. Too bad. I couldn't remember when I had felt so close to him.

6

"The Atom Smashers are the worst group in camp," said Michelle.

"I'm sure Bobby can handle six ten-year-old boys," said my mother. "Anyone ready for another piece of chicken?"

"It's delicious," said my father, holding out his plate. "Who makes up those names, Atom Smashers?"

"At Opening Day Ceremonies, each group decided on its own name," said Michelle. "The counselor and five of the boys voted for Rumson Rangers. The sixth boy wanted Atom Smashers."

"Nothing like democracy in action," I said.

"Laugh while you can," said Michelle. "That sixth boy was Harley Bell."

"That redheaded . . ."

"Bobby!" warned my mother.

"Why are you always so sure I'm going to say a dirty word?" I asked. "I think you've got a dirty mind."

"Robert!" My father glared at me.

"Harley Bell is a walking psychological case history," said Michelle. "He's the only male child and they treat him like a little prince. His mother died when he was born. His father is too busy making money to spend any time with him. His Uncle Moe is scared of him and his Aunt Rose dotes on him. On those rare occasions when he doesn't get exactly what he wants, he holds his breath until he turns blue."

I said, "Nothing a good shot in the chops wouldn't cure."

"There's more truth than poetry in that," said my father. "Some of these boys need to get walloped now and then just to show them somebody cares."

"Marty, that's so old-fashioned," said my mother.

"Irving would cut your hand off if you touched Harley," said Michelle. She gave me one of her phony smiles. "Lotsa luck. The first counselor lasted three days and his replacement lasted exactly one day. That's why Moe is scraping the bottom of the barrel.''

"That's not very constructive, Michelle," said my mother.

"It's all right, Mrs. Marks," I said. "Before this sibling rivalry gets out of hand, I would like to tell this earth girl the truth."

"Do I have to listen to this cretin's drivel while I'm eating?" asked Michelle.

"Fear not," I said. "My real parents will be coming for me soon."

"Is this one of your science fiction stories?" asked my father.

"I was placed here," I continued, "by the rulers of the planet Trebor, on the outer rim of the universe. Before I take my rightful place on the throne of Skram, they want me to learn humility and gain the common touch by living with some plain, decent human beings and their demented and deformed daughter."

"To-mor-row," said Michelle. It sounded like a curse. "We'll see how long *you* last with the Atom Smashers."

7

I didn't get a chance to study the Atom Smashers until we went into the casino for lunch. We had spent the morning at the waterfront and then at arts and crafts, so I had been too busy keeping Harley from drowning the other kids, and then from choking them with lanyards. Harley didn't let up for a minute. I knocked myself out trying to get between Harley and whoever he was about to clobber at the moment. I was the human shock absorber. It was tiring, but it worked, even though I couldn't pay much attention to the rest of the group. I figured lunch would be a good time to look them over. You can learn a great deal about people, even kids, by watching them eat.

Naturally, Harley Bell played with his food.

The first thing he did when we sat down at the Atom Smashers' table in the casino was to drag a slice of salami out of his sandwich and skim it across the room at one of the girls in Michelle's group, the Bluebirds. It missed her by a hair, and Michelle pretended not to notice. Michelle learned that from Mom, who taught in a pretty rough neighborhood. If you notice something, you have to react. Mom doesn't notice anything short of a switchblade knife.

"Salami stinks on hot ice," said Harley. "Third time this week."

"I like salami," said Douglas, the fattest boy in camp. "I'll eat yours."

"You'll eat anything," said Steven. He didn't say it in a nasty way, just as a matter of fact. Steven was the best athlete in the group and the natural leader.

"Here, Doug–ass," said Harley. He dragged out a second slice of salami and dropped it on the floor next to Douglas' chair. "You'll eat anything."

I couldn't ignore that. "That's disgusting," I said. I thought of Sheila making these sandwiches. I had seen her in the kitchen when we walked into the casino, but she hadn't seen me. "You know, Harley, there are starving kids all over the world who . . ."

"So mail it to them," said Harley.

"Pick it up," I said. I was surprised at how tough my voice sounded. The Atom Smashers looked at me strangely.

"You're not even a regular counselor, you're on trial," said Harley. "Pick it up yourself."

"I'll get it," said Miles. He didn't want any trouble. He was the smallest in the group, a thin boy with a serious expression.

We watched Miles pick up the salami slice, carry it across the casino to a garbage pail, and carefully drop it in. When he returned, I said, "Thank you, Miles, that was very nice."

"Thank you, Miles, that was very nice," mimicked Harley. "You little shrimp." He turned on Douglas. "Hey, whale belly. Want the rest of my sandwich?"

"Okay," said Douglas. He had already finished his lunch. The salami sandwich, the canned pears, the oatmeal cookies, the paper cup of milk, all gone. He hadn't gobbled his lunch, he had sort of inhaled it. He had leaned over his lunch, taken a deep breath, and it was gone.

"Here." Harley threw his sandwich at Douglas. It landed on his lap. The brown mustard smeared on his pants. "Look, the fat slob did it in his pants."

Barry and Larry, the identical Stern twins, giggled. They dressed exactly alike and giggled in chorus. Because I couldn't think of anything else to do, I said, "Both of you, shut up."

Barry and Larry stopped giggling.

Tears rolled down Douglas' bloated cheeks. I felt sorry for him at the same time that the sight of him disgusted me. He might have been as fat as I was at ten years old.

"Stop sniveling, Douglas," I said.

"Here," said Miles. He handed Douglas one of his cookies. Douglas thanked him and inhaled it. He kept on crying.

"Hey, hippo," said Harley, "I'm going to do you a favor." He dug into his pants pocket. "I'm going to melt off some of that blubber." He pulled out a wooden kitchen match.

"That's a match," said Steven.

"You're a real Einstein," said Harley. He

whipped the match across the tabletop. It exploded into flame. "Okay, blob, your troubles are over."

"Put that out," I roared.

In the sudden silence I heard the whisper of the flame. There was no other sound in the casino. Campers and counselors sat frozen at their tables, food suspended in midair.

"Make me," said Harley.

I thought of Hemingway's moment of truth, when the bull is charging across the arena and you've got to face the horns or run.

I leaned across the table and slapped the match out of his hand.

Harley jumped up and ran out of the casino. A few campers cheered.

"Maybe he'll get run over by a car," said either Barry or Larry, hopefully.

The other said, "Maybe he'll get run over by a car."

By the time I got outside, Harley was shimmying up a drainpipe to the roof of the casino. When he got there he looked down at me and slapped the crook of his right arm with his left hand. When I was ten I didn't even know what that meant.

"Get down here," I said.

"Come and get me."

"Oh, no," groaned Moe Bell, rushing up. "Irving is going to have a fit." He grabbed my arm. "What did you do to the boy?"

"He was going to burn another camper."

"Never, not Harley." Moe looked up. "Come on down, have an ice cream."

"What flavor?"

"You pick."

"Pistachio."

"Come on, Harley," said Moe, "don't be difficult."

"All right. Chocolate." Harley started hopping on the roof.

"Okay. But first you've got to sit down," Bubbles of sweat broke out on Moe's bald head. "Where's Sheila?"

"I'll go get . . ."

"No, Bobby, I want you to run to the store, fast as you can, bring back a couple of chocolate Dixie cups. On the double now."

I took off, just as a crowd began to form under

Harley. The little rat was grinning and waving. I heard Moe send Al for a ladder, and shout for Sheila.

There was nobody in the general store. The top of the fridge was loaded with ice pops and Dixie cups, all of them encrusted with gray ice. I wondered if they were a kind of submarine, too. It took a couple of minutes to chop out two chocolate cups.

"What are you doing here?" asked Rose Bell. I hadn't heard her come in.

"Harley's on the roof of the casino, he . . ."

"Oh, no," she groaned. "Go, go, don't just stand there." I ran all the way back, the Dixie cups softening in my hot hands. Moe had sent everyone back into the casino. A rickety wooden ladder was set against the edge of the roof. Harley was sitting down, peeling tiles off the roof.

"Here, give me those," said Moe, grabbing the Dixie cups. He held them up to Harley. "Here's your ice cream. Come on down."

"I want 'em up here."

"Harley, your father will be very angry . . ."

"At you, you skinhead," said Harley. "Now give me my ice cream."

"Will you come down after you eat it?"

"I'll think about it."

"I know you'll do the right thing." Moe tossed up one of the Dixie cups. "Harley, enjoy."

Harley ripped off the round paper cover, folded it, and scooped out a melting brown glob.

"Bobby." Moe's face was next to mine. "You stay here, watch him . . ."

"My group . . ."

"Your group." The *p* nearly blew my head off. "You'll be lucky if you have a job at Happy Valley when this day is over, letting Harley . . ."

"He might have burned . . ."

"I don't want to hear your excuses, I want results. Now. I'll be back as soon as I get the afternoon activities organized. I want you to watch him like a hawk. If he falls off the roof, you catch him."

"Catch him?" I couldn't believe it.

"At least break his fall with your body." Moe handed me the other Dixie cup and hurried away.

As soon as he was gone, Harley began scraping his heels on the pebbly, gray asphalt roof

62

tiles. "I'm falling, I'm falling, catch me, catch me." His laugh sounded like a dog's bark. "Gimme the other ice cream."

I tossed it up to him and leaned against the ladder. His red hair glinted in the noon sun. Behind him, a chicken hawk circled slowly in a pale blue sky. I tracked the bird as it swooped down, stalled, then soared.

"What are you looking at?"

"A buzzard," I said. "In case it attacks you."

"You're making that up."

"Believe what you want." I watched the hawk until it became a black dot.

"Buzzards don't attack people."

"They have bad eyesight," I said. "They make mistakes. They might think a kid with red hair is a wounded red fox or even a red pony with a broken leg." Imagination, I thought, where would a writer be without it?

"A red pony?"

"Sure. One time a buzzard stuck its beak right into the eye of a red pony."

"You're making that up." He slid closer to the edge of the roof.

"No, I'm not." I wasn't. It came from *The*

Red Pony, one of my favorite stories by John Steinbeck. I quoted from memory. "'The first buzzard sat on the pony's head and its beak had just risen dripping with dark eye fluid.'"

I heard a soft scraping noise behind me, but I didn't dare turn away and break the mood. I had Harley mesmerized, staring into my face, his blue eyes wide and frightened.

"What would you do if the buzzards attack?" he asked.

"I'd call your Uncle Moe. He'd go get a shotgun."

"That could take a long time."

"Probably." I shielded my eyes with my hand and searched the sky. Not even a sparrow. "There's a couple, but they're nothing to worry about."

"Would you get the shotgun now?" His lower lip was trembling, in fact all of his mean little face was coming apart. "Please don't let them get me. Not in the eyes."

"Come on down. You won't be such a target on the ground."

"Hold the ladder for me?"

It was that simple. His legs quivered as he backed slowly down the creaky ladder. When he

64

reached the ground, he turned and rushed past me. "Sheila!" he cried.

She caught his body against hers, and held his face against her chest. Her green eyes glared at me over his head. "You must be pretty proud of yourself."

"I got him down, didn't I?"

She shook her head. "Why should you know any better than his family?" She ruffled his red hair. "It's all right, Harley, nothing's going to hurt you."

"What did you want me to do?" I hated the babyish whine in my voice. Why should I care what some crabby girl thought?

"You scared him and you lied to him," she said. Her green eyes were ice chips. "What are you going to do next time?"

8

Michelle wanted to make a grand entrance at Silverstar's third annual Cocktail Party and Mixed Doubles in the Bushes so we got there an hour late. The party was in full swing. Michelle was wearing a new yellow dress that showed off her tan, and her hair, which was usually piled on top of her head, was flowing over her shoulders. She had plastered on a ton of makeup.

The moment we stepped out of the car, Jerry glided up as if he had been on the lookout for us. He carried a drink in each hand. Jerry was wearing clean white bucks, white pants, and a white V-neck pullover. I began to feel a little shabby in my tan desert boots, chinos, and blue button-down-collar shirt.

"Mi-chelle. You look fab-u-lous." He handed

us each a glass. "I hope you like your martinis dry."

Michelle sipped her martini. "Perfecto."

I sipped mine. "Just the way I like it, thanks." I had never had a martini before and I was disappointed. It was tasteless.

Jerry grabbed our elbows and steered us toward the house. "Summer rules are in effect, Brother Roberto. You mustn't do anything I wouldn't do, and after midnight, when my parents come home, you're not allowed to dance naked."

"Now you tell me," I said.

"Fun-nee." Jerry squeezed my elbow. "Michelle, you never told me your brother was such a wit."

"That's only half true," said Michelle. "He's a half-wit."

"Oh, we're all on tonight," said Jerry. "By the by, Brother Roberto, that little performance of yours at the casino roof yesterday was ab-so-lutely brilliant."

"I'm not so sure he should have lied to an emotionally disturbed child," said Michelle.

"Nonsense," said Jerry. "Life is playacting

and playacting is lying, ergo, life is lying. Don't you agree, Brother Roberto?''

Before I could answer, someone shouted "Michelle!" and a couple of girl counselors began squealing over Michelle's dress and her hair. A crowd gathered. She had gotten her grand entrance. Jerry released my elbow and nobody seemed to notice as I edged away.

The Silvers' big white house stood on a hill overlooking the south end of Rumson Lake. A thick carpet of bluegreen lawn flowed down to the shore. The lawn reminded me of Dr. Kahn's green velvet lawn, the grass I had mowed for the last two summers. After Willie Rumson set fire to his toolshed, Dr. Kahn sold his house and moved to Florida.

Thinking of Willie Rumson dried my tongue, so I gulped a mouthful of martini.

It hit me like an H-bomb. My throat stung, my chest burned, my toes curled. My head spun. The lawn swayed. I pressed the soles of my shoes against the ground and took a deep breath. The lawn stopped swaying, but it remained in a permanently tilted position. My head stopped spinning but it felt light and not too firmly attached to my neck, a balloon at the end of a thread.

Slowly, a warm feeling seeped into every nook and cranny of my body. I liked it. I smiled. I could feel the corners of my mouth lifting and stretching into an enormous smile. Why shouldn't I be happy, a witty, good-looking guy like me?

Sheila. Was she here? I began walking across the lawn, carefully because it was still tilted, looking for Sheila.

It was twilight. Couples were dancing on a stone patio under strings of colored lights that swayed in a breeze off the lake. The lights made me giggle because they were so twinkly. Each light had fuzzy little rings around it, red rings for red lights, green rings for green lights, orange rings for orange lights. The lights were hilarious.

I finished my martini. There was an olive at the bottom of the glass. I hated olives but I ate it anyway. It was delicious.

I wandered among the dancers on the patio looking for Sheila. I bumped into a few people but nobody seemed to mind. Somebody guided me around the phonograph so I wouldn't bump into that, and everybody laughed. I tried to read the words on the records but they were spinning too fast. Even the records stacked on the table were spinning too fast.

"Martooni time," called Jerry Silver. He had a pitcher in his hand. "The secret is in the vermouth," he whispered. "I don't use any." As he refilled my glass, some martini sloshed on my hand. I laughed. When I licked my hand, Jerry laughed, too.

"Easy on that stuff," said Michelle, "it's pure gin."

"I can handle my booze." I took another gulp and hung on. Only an A-bomb this time. I was getting used to it.

Al Rapp was walking along the flagstone path on his hands. It was the funniest thing I ever saw. On his hands. Were they registered as feet, too? Those mittens? I couldn't stop laughing.

"What's so funny?" asked Al, looking at me upside down. "Can you do this?"

I wanted to be nice, to say something that would make him laugh, too, so I said, "Just because you smell like ape shit doesn't mean you're Tarzan."

He flipped over and stood up. A girl got in

front of him. "Calm down, Al, can't you see he's smashed?"

"Can you do this?" yelled Al. He cartwheeled across the lawn into the darkness. I almost fell down, it was so comical.

I strolled around the house. Once I walked into a couple necking in a hammock and I apologized, turned around, and walked into a tree. I apologized.

When I passed the patio again, Jerry Silver was singing one of his big songs from *The King and I*, all about how the world was a better place when he was a boy and things were exactly what they seemed. Now that he was a man, nothing was clear anymore. I liked the song but when I stopped to listen to the words I suddenly felt dizzy and nauseous. I had to keep moving. I swallowed some more martini and pushed on. I might have walked for a half hour.

"Having a good time, Bob?" asked one of the counselors.

"Ab-sho-lutely." That cracked me up. I thought I heard myself say "ab-sho-lutely." I knew drinking could affect your speech, but your hearing, too?

The garage light was on when I circled to the back of the house this time and I walked in. A bunch of guys and girls were crowded around a Ping-Pong table. I didn't see Sheila. I was about to leave when Al Rapp shouted something at me that was drowned out by a radio blaring "Sh-Boom, Sh-Boom." I usually hated that song even worse than "Shake, Rattle, and Roll," but tonight I liked it. It was so funny.

"Ab-sho-lutely," I shouted to Al.

Someone put a Ping-Pong paddle in my hand, and said, "Al's won eight in a row."

"Next victim," said Al, waving his paddle at me.

I finished my martini and handed someone the glass. "Three and over?"

"Go ahead and serve," said Al. "I'll give you a break."

I gave him my rinky-dink cheapo slice serve which dribbles over the net and drops dead. He crashed into the table lunging for it and hit himself on the nose with his paddle. I couldn't help laughing. My rinky-dink cheapo slice hardly ever fools anyone but Mom.

I wanted to try it again, but my hand slipped

and I gave him the semiwhipper-dipper instead. It bounced off his chest. I laughed so hard someone had to pound my back to start me breathing again. Two-zip already! Shows what a martini will do for your Ping-Pong game. Or a teenie martin for your Pong-Ping game.

"Serve it up, let's go," said Al.

"Put it in his mouth, Bobby-boy," shouted some guy I had never seen before.

I held up the ball. "And now, folks, for my ipsy-dipsy A-number-one true-blue more-in-'fifty-four super whipper . . ."

"Just serve the damn ball." Al banged the edge of his paddle on the table. I felt the vibrations in my teeth.

Okay, Allie-baby, I thought, get ready for the classic serve, right out of the "Table Tennis Tips for Teens" booklet I got free for two box tops. I held the ball out on the palm of my left hand, tossed it up, and missed.

"Will you cut out that clowning and play," yelled Al.

He thought I missed purposely! I couldn't remember when I had heard anything so humorous.

"And stop that cackling."

73

"Take it easy, Al," said a girl. "It's just a game."

"So then let's play it. Somebody shut off that radio."

I stopped laughing long enough to serve a nice fat one that bounced high and easy on Al's side. He licked his lips as he got set for the kill.

Thuk. He whacked the ball so hard he crushed it in midair. It plopped in front of him. My stomach ached from laughing so hard and tears rolled down my cheeks.

Someone handed me a new ball and I served again. Another easy fat one. This time Al stroked it smoothly back to me.

I watched it come, nice and slow. There were two balls. Both twinkly. Just like the colored lights. So cute. I decided to swing at the one on the left. Nothing happened. Wrong choice.

"I quit," said Al. He slammed his paddle down on the table. "I came to play, not jerk around." He stalked out of the garage.

One of the girls snatched up his paddle. "I'm next." She was holding two paddles. Twinkly ones. And her face was out of focus.

"I'm retiring," I announced. "Undefeated." I

gave away my paddle. "Undefeated Ping-Pong king of Rumson Lake. I'm the Ping-Pong King-Kong."

Someone cheered as I stumbled out of the garage. I think it was me.

This time when I passed the patio, everybody was playing charades. They were laughing and jumping around. That gave me a headache. I found a half-filled martini glass on a little table under a tree. I was so thirsty I gulped it down.

The lawn pitched me against the tree. I sat down. I felt dizzier. I put my face into the grass and closed my eyes.

When I opened my eyes the lawn was calm. From somewhere in the darkness I heard Michelle sing "Hello, Young Lovers."

I followed her voice down to the lake.

She was standing on the Silvers' private dock, as if it was a stage. A dozen people were sitting in a semicircle on the grass listening to her.

I sat down a few feet behind them.

"Sounds good, doesn't she?" asked Jerry, sitting next to me.

"Ummm-huh." A sour fluid was rising in my

throat and I was afraid it would spill out if I opened my mouth.

"Do you sing?"

"Uh-uh."

"You should come out for the show anyway. There are three good nonsinging roles, Captain Orton, Sir Edward Ramsey, and The Kralahome. You get to wear a loincloth for that one." He squeezed my leg. "I think you've got the muscles for it."

"I'm no actor."

"After the roof? We heard it all through a window. You were superb." His hand was still on my leg.

I moved sideways and slid my leg out from under his hand.

Jerry said, "You can audition privately if you're nervous."

I jumped up and ran toward the house. I stumbled over bodies in the darkness. Voices cursed at me but I kept going, stumbling, falling, pushing people out of my way until I reached the patio. A few couples were dancing, very slowly, very close.

I couldn't stop shivering. There was a portable

bar in a corner of the patio. The martini pitcher stood on a tray surrounded by used glasses. I poured a drink and swallowed it. I held on to the bar as my body shuddered.

"Bob? Are you all right?" Through the ringing in my ears I couldn't recognize the voice. Was it Jerry?

I ran.

"Bob?"

I plunged into the woods behind the house. Low branches whipped my face. Twice I tripped on roots and fell sprawling. I climbed over a fence. My pants snagged on barbed wire. I ripped them loose.

My stomach heaved. I bent over to vomit but nothing came up. A dog growled, came closer, then scampered away.

I was in a field, running. The wind was cool in my damp hair. The faster I ran, the more nauseous I felt. When I slowed, my face began to burn. Footsteps echoed behind me. Was he coming after me? I ran faster, stopping only to retch.

Suddenly, gravel crunched under my feet. Headlights flared in my face. I was running along the shoulder of the county road. How did I get out here? Through the fog in my head I thought, As long as I keep the lake on my left I'll be headed toward home.

A car whooshed past, screeched to a stop, stormed backward.

"Marks?"

"Leave me alone."

"It's me. Jim."

A girl's voice. "What a mess."

Another girl. "Doesn't smell so hot either."

I was being pushed into the backseat. A couple moved away to make room. "He really tied one on." They all laughed.

"It's all right, Marks. Just relax."

I passed out. When I opened my eyes again we were in my driveway. Jim Smith and another guy were pulling me out of the car.

The light over my front door went on.

My mother's voice. "Who's there?"

"You take it easy now, Marks." Jim aimed me toward the front door and gave me a little shove. "Leave the serious drinking for thems who can hold it."

I staggered toward the light. Doors slammed

behind me and the car burned rubber pulling away.

"Bobby! Are you all right?" My mother stood in the doorway.

"Ab-sho-lutely."

My father appeared beside her. "What the hell were you doing with those characters? Didn't I tell you . . ."

Then the front steps rose up to smack me in the face.

9

I got out of bed very slowly on Sunday morning. My legs were rubbery. The back of my head ached and there was a sickly, hollow feeling in the pit of my stomach. I staggered to the bathroom, holding on to furniture and walls and doorknobs along the way. I splashed ice-cold water on my face and the back of my neck. I rinsed out the cotton taste in my mouth.

When I felt strong enough to take the shock I looked at myself in the mirror. Not so bad. My eyes were puffy and my upper lip was swollen where the front steps had slugged it, but otherwise I looked fine, Big Bob Marks, bloody but unbowed after another Saturday night laughing and brawling in the hellholes and the hot spots.

At least now I'd be able to write about a hangover without faking it.

I couldn't understand why everyone looked so glum when I finally shambled out to the dining room. Mom and Dad and Michelle were sitting in front of empty coffee cups. The Sunday newspapers were still in a neat pile.

"How are you feeling, Bobby?" asked my mother.

Before I could come up with a snappy answer, my father said, "You are beached."

"Beached?"

"Grounded. You can forget about driving this summer."

"Why?"

"Don't you play dumb with me." The little bad news muscles were twitching along his jaw.

"Okay, I got drunk," I said. "It won't happen again."

"You bet it won't," said my father. "Until further notice, Robert, your curfew is nine o'clock."

"Is that A.M. or P.M.?" It just slipped out.

My father slammed his hand on the table so

hard that the coffee cups rattled and two bagels jumped off their plate.

"Marty!"

"We have never been strict enough with this boy." My father spoke through his teeth. He did not look at me. "Forget the curfew. When you return from camp at five . . . P.M. . . . you will proceed directly to your room and stay there until it is time to go back to camp the next morning. You may leave your room only for supper, breakfast and to use the bathroom."

"For how long?"

"Until I tell you otherwise."

"That's not fair." I turned to Mom and Michelle for support. Nothing. Mom looked sad and concerned, and Michelle looked tense. "It was the first time. I didn't do it on purpose. I didn't know how strong that stuff was."

"You shouldn't have been drinking in the first place," said my father. "At your age . . ."

"You were sixteen," I said.

"What?"

"Grandma told me, that time at Uncle Harold's wedding when you went around to every table and finished the wine in every glass . . ."

"I don't believe how he's twisting this, Lenore."

"Sit down, Marty."

". . . they had to carry you home, you were drunk as a skunk, that's Grandma's exact words, drunk as a skunk . . ."

Crack!

I turned my head at the last instant and his open hand slapped my ear. Bells rang.

"You go right to your room now, I don't want to see your face for the rest of the day." His eyes were wild and his cheeks were as white as the belly of a fish. I got scared. "You deliberately disobeyed me, you defied me, and I don't know when I'll trust you again."

"Wait a minute, I didn't . . ."

"I hope you enjoyed your night out with those Rummies because, it's going to be your last night out for a long, long . . ."

"Hey, wait a minute, I wasn't . . ."

"Get out of my sight."

"They brought me home, that's all."

"OUT!"

I left the room in a hurry. You can't talk to him when he's bellowing like that and I didn't want to give him another shot at my head.

Besides, when he gets so mad that the blood drains out of his face I'm always afraid he'll have a heart attack or burst a blood vessel. I wouldn't want it to be my fault.

I closed my door and put my nonringing ear to it. I heard Michelle's voice but I couldn't make out what she was saying. I felt a little better. Michelle could straighten it out. Dad wasn't so mad that I came home drunk, he was mad because he thought I had gone out with Jim Smith against his orders. I could understand that—drinking plus driving could add up to a Rummie car crash with me in it.

But Michelle would tell them how I got drunk at Jerry's party, and then he'd believe that Jim Smith had picked me up on the road. I'd have to come up with a convincing reason for leaving the party. I could say I was looking for Michelle to drive me home and in my drunken stupor I wandered out to the county road. That might do it. I certainly couldn't tell them the truth. Even if I was sure what the truth was. Had Jerry really made a pass at me? Had I imagined it or misinterpreted it in my drunkenness?

"Bobby?" Michelle was carrying a tray. Orange

juice, bagels with cream cheese and lox, a tall glass of milk and a wedge of crumb cake. Good old Michelle, I knew she'd come through.

"How'd he take it? When you told him what really happened."

She put the tray on my knees. "I knew you'd be starving."

"Didn't you tell him?"

She didn't look at me. "It'll be all right. You know he never stays angry for long."

"You go right out there and tell him the truth."

"You're spilling your milk." She snatched the tray off my knees and gave me a phony smile. "I think we're both capable of a rational discussion."

"About what? You told him the truth or you didn't."

She looked at me slyly. "You lied to Harley Bell."

"To get him off the roof. That was different."

"Was it? In other words, you're telling me, there are times when lying is permissible. When it's in a good cause, right?"

"Look, I'm in no mood for a Barn-yard College bull session. Just give me the facts."

"Okay. Dad thinks you snuck out of Jerry's party early to meet Jim Smith. That you set it up in advance."

"You know that's not true."

"Do I?" She shrugged. "I don't know when you left the party. You certainly didn't inform me."

For a moment I actually considered telling her about Jerry's hand on my leg. Better not. She'd come up with a psychological analysis. She'd tell me that I imagined the whole thing because I really *wanted* Jerry to put his hand on my leg.

"Look, it's really very simple. I got drunk and the next thing I knew I was on the county road. Jim picked me up."

"I believe you," she said, "but I don't think I can convince Dad. And maybe it's better he thinks you got drunk with the Rummies."

"But he'll think that I purposely disobeyed him and he'll hate Jim even more than he . . ."

"So what? Nothing's going to improve his opinion of the Smiths and the Rumsons. One more mark against them won't matter."

"Sure, let's turn 'em in as Reds, too, stealing atomic secrets . . ."

"Consider the alternative," said Michelle. "If Mom and Dad think you got pie-eyed at Jerry's party, they'll never trust the counselors at Happy Valley, either. There are seven more weeks of camp, with parties and cookouts and . . ."

"You fink," I shouted. "You're just afraid they'll beach *you* when they find out the kind of people you . . ."

"Shhhh. Look, Bobby, nobody sat on your chest and poured gin down your throat. You were the big shot guzzling that stuff. I told you to take it easy, didn't I?"

I calmed down. "So?"

"So relax." She put the tray back on my knees. "Let them think the Rummies got you drunk. You might meet somebody you like at camp and want to go back at night."

I thought of Sheila. "But Dad said I had to . . ."

"He'll get over that in a few days. I'll work on him when the time's right."

"And the car?"

"You'll be driving with him again in a few days. I promise."

I looked her in the eye. She didn't blink.

Michelle was tricky, but when she promised she usually came through. Besides, she didn't want Mom and Dad to think Jerry was a bad influence. I had something on her.

"You've really got Dad wrapped around your pinkie, don't you?"

She winked. "Thank your lucky stars, Brother Roberto."

10

On Monday morning, when Jerry Silver walked out of the arts and crafts shack when I walked in, I got the feeling he was avoiding me. But I couldn't be one hundred percent sure—everybody walked away from the Atom Smashers.

I had no time to stew about it. Harley was up to his usual nasty tricks and I had my hands full. He tripped little kids and he threw food and he disrupted activities. Like all true bullies, he picked his victims with care. So it was open season on Douglas and Miles.

At least five times a day he would walk up to Miles, usually when the little guy was standing with other campers to make the humiliation worse, and shout, "Where's Miles? Where'd he go?"

Harley would make a big show of circling

Miles, looking around him, over his head and behind him, while shouting, "Where is he? You need a magnifying glass to find him. He's so little you need a microscope."

After the first couple of times, nobody laughed. And Miles never reacted. Stone face. He pretended he never heard it. I couldn't tell if Miles was just so tough inside he didn't care, or if he was secretly crying his heart out and didn't want anyone to know. A few times I squeezed his shoulder and told him not to let it bother him, and he looked at me as if he didn't know what I was talking about.

Douglas would begin reacting as soon as Harley looked his way. His lips would twist and his eyes would fill with tears. By the time Harley got around to calling him "Fatso" and "Lardass" and "Tubs," Douglas' face looked like a melting candle.

Harley's favorite way of embarrassing Douglas was to wait for someone to ask, "Did you see the volleyball?" or "Where are the extra folding chairs?" This would happen several times a day, and Harley would shout, "Douglas ate them."

Then he would rush over to Douglas, pat him

on the stomach, and yell, "Here's the volleyball."

After a while, watching Douglas just stand there and melt, I stopped feeling sorry for him. All he had to do was reach out and punch Harley. Or grab him and sit on him. Once, in a very subtle way so I couldn't be blamed, I suggested to Douglas that he could solve his problem with one swift kick. Douglas looked at me as blankly as Miles did.

I spent so much time shadowing Harley that I wasn't much of a counselor to the five other boys in my group. I brought that up at dinner one night with Michelle and Mom. Dad was back in the city, working.

"Have you spoken to Moe about Harley?" asked Mom. "After all, he is a professional educator."

"Moe doesn't want to hear about it," said Michelle. "Harley's a blind spot with him."

"Who takes care of Harley at night and on the weekends?" asked Mom.

"They brought up a cousin from the city," said Michelle. "Poor kid, they make her work in the kitchen during the day and baby-sit Harley the rest of the time."

"You mean Sheila?" I asked.

"You know her?" asked Michelle.

"I . . . uh, talked to her last week. Do you know her? What's she like?"

Michelle shrugged. "Who knows? She sounds like she's from the depths of Brooklyn."

"Listen to the queen of the Ivy League," I said.

"Go suck a rock." Michelle stood up. "It's your turn to help with the dishes tonight." She strutted off for a quick plaster-and-paint job on her face before she left to rehearse with Jerry.

"There is another aspect to all this," said Mom. "The problem child crying out for attention often needs your help and energy more than the others."

"There's another counselors' meeting on Friday night. I'm going to try to bring it up, no matter what Michelle says."

"I'm proud of you, taking it all so seriously," said Mom. "But you do look tired."

"I am. It's a different kind of tiredness from mowing lawns. A meal and a shower don't make me feel better. I'm going to bed after the dishes."

"Why don't you go on to bed now? I'll finish up here."

"That's not fair, it's my turn . . ."

She stood up and came around the table to kiss me on top of my head. "You're excused."

I didn't put up much of a fight. "Thanks." On my way out I staggered a little extra so Mom would know she was doing the right thing. But not so much that she would worry about me.

As soon as I sat down on my bed to undress, I realized how tired I was. I barely had the strength to untie my sneakers. Was I doomed to six more weeks of this sickly kind of tired? My eyes burned even when I closed them, I had a headache that blotted out any good lines or story ideas I might think of, and my neck and back hurt all the time.

The last two summers, I'd come home hurting after a day of mowing lawns, but it was a good, healthy pain, all my muscles complaining they were overworked, the soles of my feet and the palms of my hands rubbed raw. Under that pain I could feel myself growing stronger and harder and leaner, and my soles and palms turning tough with calluses. And the next morning I was ready to do it all over again.

And in those days my mind, my imagination, my dream machine, was never tired for a minute, it was always fresh and ready to streak across the universe or plunge down into the deepest, darkest, scariest secret thought.

Nowadays my brain felt as weak and washed out as the rest of me by five P.M. And Moe hadn't mentioned raising my salary back to the original contract. One problem at a time.

I switched on the radio. "Sh-Boom." It reminded me of the garage and Ping-Pong and Al and martinis and Jerry, everything I wanted to forget. I spun the dial until I tuned in Teresa Brewer singing "Till I Waltz Again With You." I fell asleep thinking about Sheila.

11

Moe Bell dumped a pile of shriveled hot dogs next to a heap of stale buns on a picnic table, along with a haystack of dry coleslaw left over from a week of camp lunches, a case of orange soda-bottle submarines and a few torn bags of rocky marshmallows. That was his idea of a cookout for his counselors. And he wouldn't let us near the food until after we held our meeting.

Not that I could have eaten anyway. Sheila was there, a bright red scarf tied around her curly black hair. As corny as it sounds, the moment I saw her my heart skipped a beat. Sometimes you just can't do better than a cliché.

Moe arranged us sitting in a circle on a grassy clearing just above the sandy beach of the water-front area. It was very quiet with the kids gone home. The bright yellow sun of the camp day had softened to the gentle orange of late afternoon. The mildest of breezes stirred Rumson Lake and the leaves of the trees along the shore. I wondered what it would be like here alone with Sheila. When I sneaked a look at her across the circle, our eyes met. She had been sneaking a look at me! I turned away so fast I got a crick in my neck.

Moe clapped for attention. "This meeting is what the highfalutin' eggheads at the Board of Education call a 'Primary Evaluation Conference.' I call it a 'Let-your-hair-down session.'" He tapped his bald head and laughed. So did all the counselors in the circle, except Sheila. When I saw the contemptuous expression on her face, I choked off my own laugh.

"There are only two rules," continued Moe. "Don't insult anyone and don't say anything that isn't one hundred percent true.

"Now," he looked around the circle, "you can say anything you want, you can take anyone to task, including poor ol' Moe, you can criticize any aspect of camp policy. Fire away."

No one said a word. Al began rubbing a

muscle in his pinkie. Those great sophisticates, the King of Siam and Anna, rolled their eyes at each other. The other counselors stared at the ground under their crossed legs or cleared their throats or scratched themselves.

"Does this mean everything's perfect?" asked Moe.

I looked at Sheila. Was that an almost imperceptible nod of her head? A signal for me to speak? I started talking before I started thinking.

"This isn't a criticism, it's more like a comment," I said. Every head in the circle turned in my direction. I glimpsed Michelle's face twisted with pain. What did she think I was going to say?

"Feel free, Bobby," said Moe, encouragingly.

"It's about Harley."

There were groans around the circle. Sheila's green eyes narrowed. The smile on Moe's face shrank into a thin line. "What about Harley?"

"Taking care of him is a full-time job," I said, "and I . . ."

"If you can't handle it . . ."

". . . feel I'm cheating the rest of the group . . ."

". . . we can find someone who can." Moe's voice was cold.

"You said I should feel free."

"But not to insult me," said Moe. "You violated rule number one."

"How did I insult you?"

"You know very well how you insulted me," said Moe.

"No, I don't."

"That's not one hundred percent true," said Moe. "By saying you don't know, you just violated rule number two."

This was crazy. I looked around the circle for support. Michelle was shaking her head angrily at me and Al was flexing the muscles in his scalp and Jerry was arching his eyebrows over closed eyes. Sheila looked as though she was trying not to laugh. Some of the others looked puzzled, and some looked bored.

"Now that Bobby's broken the ice," said Moe, "who else has something to say?"

The waterfront counselor raised her hand and proceeded to chew out all of us except Moe for goofing off during free swims. Then Al squawked about counselors not making their kids return the bats and balls from the softball field. The arts and crafts counselor announced that two of her leather punches were missing, and Michelle complained that boys from the Eagles group were spying on her Bluebirds while they changed clothes at the lake. Really important stuff.

"Well," said Moe, finally, "we all feel a lot better now, don't we?" He nodded his head, and swept the circle with his eyes until everyone else was nodding. He stood up. "Okay, gang, it's party time, courtesy of the Bell family, and I'm going to get out of your way since I don't have any more hair to let down." He kept tapping his head until everybody was laughing except Sheila and me. Then, with a scowl for me, he walked away.

"Nice going, Bigmouth," said Michelle. "I told you Harley was his blind spot."

"Easy on the lad," said Jerry. "He still thinks that camp is for campers."

Al yelled, "I got some beer stashed in the . . ."

"Sit still," snapped the waterfront counselor. "Last year after the cookout there was garbage on the beach and I found a broken bottle in the shallow area. It could have slashed a kid's foot.

We need a cleanup committee, a few people to take complete responsibility for policing up the waterfront area.''

"Let the girls do it," shouted Al.

The waterfront counselor got a wicked grin on her face. "We'll all race out to the far raft and back. Last two swimmers clean up."

"That's not fair," wailed Al.

"Might as well use those muscles for something useful," said the waterfront counselor. "Let's go."

Everybody began stripping down to their bathing suits. Sheila was wearing a tight, shiny blue number. She was really built, a big bust and a thin waist and cute backside. But she was as pale as she had been the first day of the summer. After two weeks, she was the only one without a suntan.

"Ready?" bawled the waterfront counselor.

We all rushed down to the edge of the beach for the start. I found myself next to Al.

"I'm gonna get that broad someday," he was yammering to anyone who would listen. "She knows my muscle density pulls me down. I can't float because there isn't an ounce of fat on me."

"What about your head?" asked Jerry.

"Rotate," said Al, giving Jerry the finger. "GO!"

I hit the water in a flat racing dive and went right into an Australian crawl. I took a breath every fourth stroke and I didn't look around until I reached the near raft, the one for beginning swimmers. I was keeping up with the waterfront counselor. Everyone else was behind us. Al was way behind us, his head bobbing on the water as he tried to run along the bottom of the lake.

Without missing a stroke, the waterfront counselor shouted to me, "Where'd you get such good form?"

I was so flattered that I stopped to answer, like a jerk. She shot away from me like a torpedo and she kicked water into my face. I swallowed a mouthful. By the time I was swimming again, she was on her way to the far raft and other counselors were catching up to me. Someday I'm gonna get that broad, too.

I had lost a lot of momentum, and two guys passed me before I reached the far raft, the halfway point of the race. There was no way I could win now, or even come in second, but since there wasn't much chance of losing either, I stopped to tread water and check out the field. The waterfront counselor had made her turn around the far raft and she was on her way back to shore, so far ahead that she was taunting everyone by swimming in a lazy backstroke. The two guys who had passed me were chasing her in vain.

Behind me, Jerry, who was a pretty good swimmer, was leading two girl counselors. They weren't killing themselves. Behind them came Sheila, who was churning away and not going too fast.

Michelle, who was right behind Sheila, could have passed her anytime she wanted to. Michelle was a very good swimmer, but she was doing a slow breaststroke so she could keep her head above water. She didn't want to get her hair wet tonight. Michelle was like that. She turned on the speed only when she had to.

There were two more girls behind Michelle and then Al brought up the rear. He was dog-paddling along, huffing and puffing and spouting water like Moby Dick.

One of the girls swimming with Jerry said, "You all right, Bob?"

"Sure."

"Why'd you stop?"

That's when I got my brainstorm. "Just a little leg cramp," I said, grabbing onto the ladder of the raft. "Be okay in a minute."

Jerry and the two girls swam around the raft and headed toward shore. The waterfront counselor was already on the beach, drying her hair with a towel. Sheila splashed up.

"What's wrong?" she gasped.

"Slow down," I said.

"Nothing doing, I don't . . ." Then, like telepathy, she got the brainstorm, too. She grabbed the ladder and smiled at me.

Michelle stroked up smoothly. "What's the matter?"

"Slight cramps, nothing serious," I said.

"Both of you?"

"It's contagious," said Sheila.

Michelle sniffed. "I couldn't care less." She breaststroked past us.

Sheila's eyes were dancing with excitement. My stomach was fluttering. The last two girl counselors passed us. Sheila pointed her nose toward Al. "Here comes Moby Dick."

"You mean The Great White Snail?"

We both started laughing at the same time, and whenever we looked at each other we laughed harder. Once I lost my grip on the ladder and slipped underwater and continued laughing, and I must have swallowed half the lake before I came up again, laughing and choking. By the time we had calmed down to giggles, Al had paddled up.

"You two quit?"

"Cramps," said Sheila.

He sneered at me. "Wise guys always get it in the end." He paddled on.

We held our breaths until he made the turn, and then we exploded with laughter again. We laughed and looked at each other and laughed some more. I couldn't remember when I had laughed so much and felt so good. Lighter than air. The king of the lake.

Finally, we were even out of giggles. Nothing left but smiles.

"Let's go in," I said. "We've clinched our defeat."

I waited for Sheila to set the pace, then timed my stroke to hers. I kicked underwater, just enough to keep my legs from sinking. I didn't want to splash away the mood.

We swam side by side, never speaking or touching or looking into each other's eyes, but I felt as though I was holding her in my arms, as if we were just one person, gliding through the water, alone in a world of soft waves caressing our bodies and gentle breezes combing our hair and a darkening blue sky that concealed and protected us.

It was over too soon.

"Here comes the garbage detail," shouted Al.

By the way some of the counselors grinned at Sheila and me as we came out of the water, I could tell we hadn't conned everybody with our strategy. I couldn't care less. In a few hours, when they all left, I'd be alone with Sheila. Here. On the soft grass by the side of a lake in the moonlight.

The next couple of hours lasted a year. I ran around collecting more wood for the fire. I helped fork out coleslaw. I handed out the beer bottles Al had hidden from Moe in a net bag in the water. Every few minutes I dashed into the bushes to pee, I was so nervous. I sharpened twigs for marshmallow roasting. I ran all the way back up to the casino to fetch Jerry's guitar. I boosted the waterfront counselor up Al's back so she could hand stand on his shoulders. I did everything I could think of to kill time except eat and look at Sheila. I had no appetite for food and I couldn't look at Sheila without breaking into the world's silliest grin. I did notice that she was eating a lot, though.

I thought that cookout would never end. Jerry seemed to know the words of every song ever written, especially Broadway show tunes, and he was ready to sing them all in one night. I silently cursed anyone who requested another song or threw another branch on the campfire and I silently cheered every time another counselor stood up and said good night and shuffled off into the darkness.

Sheila and I sat together in the circle around the fire, but we didn't hold hands or even touch. We didn't speak to each other. Sometimes our shoulders brushed and I thought I felt her body quiver. Mine did. Could she be as excited as I was?

Jerry and Michelle were the last to leave. They had been sitting back to back, like bookends without books. They tried to stand up back to back, without using their hands, couldn't make it and, laughing, helped each other up. They seemed so close. I was glad I hadn't told anyone about Jerry's hand on my leg. I must have been mistaken.

They started to walk away, then Michelle turned. "Bobby? How are you getting home?"

"He'll fly on gossamer wings," said Jerry. "C'mon, Michelle, can't you tell when you're not wanted?" I silently cheered as he led her away.

Suddenly, we were alone. I trembled. I felt shy.

"How *are* you getting home?" asked Sheila.

"I'll walk."

"It's a couple of miles."

"That's nothing."

"Don't you have a car?"

I wasn't about to tell her I was sixteen years old going into my senior year in high school and

I didn't even have a license to drive in the daytime yet. I said, "Car's in the shop. I nearly wrecked it."

"A bad accident?" she asked.

"One of those things," I murmured.

"You don't have to talk about it if you don't want to," she said.

"Thanks. Let's clean up."

"There isn't all that much to do." Sheila switched on a flashlight and swept the beach and the grassy clearing with the beam. The counselors had thrown most of their garbage in the refuse barrel, and someone had taken away the soda bottles for return deposits. We picked up a few crumpled napkins and half-eaten hamburger buns.

I wished there was more. After waiting so long to be alone with her, I suddenly wasn't sure what to do next.

"Let's sit over there," said Sheila.

I followed her to a thick old tree at the edge of the clearing. We sat side by side and leaned against the trunk. I wondered how to put my arm around her. Should I start moving it up slowly, inch by inch, then slide it across the back of her shoulders, or should I just throw it on her in one bold motion?

I didn't like either technique so I kept my hands cupped on my knees.

She had picked the best spot to sit. The moonlight filtered between the trees and cast a shimmering glow on the waterfront area. The grassy clearing was now a pale green pool and the sandy beach was a bone-white desert. The two rafts bobbed gently on the water. Beyond them, in the middle of Rumson Lake, was the forbidden Eden of Make-Out Island.

The only sound was the creaking of the camp rowboat as it strained against the chain that moored it to a tree. Some night that boat might carry the two of us to the island, I thought.

We sat in silence for a long time. When I finally cleared my throat to talk, we spoke simultaneously.

I said, "I thought you were mad at me. . . ."

And she said, "I liked the way you stood up to Moe. . . ."

We laughed and I put my arm around her. Without thinking. It was that natural. And she leaned against me and put her cheek on my collarbone. I wondered if she could hear my heart trying to hammer through my ribs.

"You're not mad at me anymore for lying to Harley?"

"You got him off the roof—I guess that was the important thing."

"But you were right about not lying to kids. Then they'll never trust you," I said.

"But you had to get him off before he got hurt," she said. "And you did it."

"Maybe there could've been a better way."

"He's so difficult sometimes," she said. "He's been through a lot. It isn't all his fault the way he acts."

"Do you spend a lot of time with him?"

She sighed. "Whenever he's not in camp he's my responsibility."

"It must be hell."

"Not really. He listens to me. Moe thinks it's because I look like Harley's mother. Or at least the pictures Harley has of her. Hey . . . do we have to talk about Harley now?"

"It's nice here, isn't it?" I said quickly.

"It's my favorite place. I love the way the moonlight comes through the trees."

I felt a twinge of jealousy. Did she come here with other guys? "You come here a lot?"

"Sometimes."

"Nothing like this in Brooklyn," I said. I wanted to sound cool, as if I didn't care too much. After all, she came here with a lot of other guys. What did they do? How far did they go?

"How should I know? I'm from the Bronx."

I felt like a complete dork. Why was I trying to start a fight, ruin the evening? She probably came here alone. I tried to make up. "There are lots of nice places in the Bronx."

"Name one," she said.

"Speaking of names, I really like yours. Sheila Bell. It's onomatopoetic."

"What are you talking about?" She lifted her head off my chest.

"Onomatopeia is when a word sounds like what it's supposed to be describing." I gave a silent cheer for Eleventh Grade Honors English. You never know when that stuff comes in handy. "Sheila Bell. Sheila Bell. You can almost hear the ringing echoes."

"Bob?" It was the first time she ever said my name. "Yeah?" I turned toward her.

Her face was an inch from mine. I felt her breath on my skin. It was warm and it smelled sweet.

We kissed.

When we broke for air, thunder roared in my ears and fires raged over my body.

We pressed each other and kissed again until the world exploded in blinding lights and rattling screams.

"So there you are," cawed Rose Bell.

12

"You're back in the driver's seat today," said my father, "because you didn't lie to me. I can forgive a mistake, perhaps even a deliberate act of disobedience, but lying is never justified. Don't you agree?"

"Ummmmha," I said, which I figured was neither a lie nor the truth. I was glad I didn't have to look him in the eye. I was staring at the empty road ahead as I tore along Drag Alley at the incredible speed of twenty miles per hour.

My father said, "As Shakespeare wrote, 'Oh, what a tangled web we weave, when first we practice to deceive.'"

It was Sir Walter Scott, not Shakespeare. We had studied that in Honors English. But I wasn't about to correct him. Very carefully, I asked,

"Just for argument's sake, aren't there times when a lie could be a good thing?"

"Such as?"

"Let's say Michelle's got a heavy date. She asks you how she looks. She's got bags under her eyes and a red nose from a cold and her chin's all broken out with pimples.

"Should you tell her the truth, that she looks awful, and spoil her evening? Or should you tell her a little lie so she won't feel so self-conscious?"

"That's not a good example." He chuckled. "You know Michelle wouldn't even answer the telephone if she had a pimple."

Michelle was a lot tougher than that, but I wasn't going to argue with him about his little Snow White. After all, she had talked him into giving me another chance.

"Let's say it's not Michelle."

"Make a U-turn here."

I slowed to a complete stop, checked my rear- and sideview mirrors twice, stuck my head out the window to look up and down the road, and into the sky for small planes landing, before I made my U-turn at five miles per hour.

"Very well done," said my father. "You may take her up to twenty-five."

What a thrill! I accelerated slowly and eased off as the needle reached 25 on the speedometer. A farmer's pickup truck pulled out of a side road, roared up behind us, and passed as if we were parked.

"Damn cowboy," snorted my father.

I never did know when to quit when I was ahead. "Don't you think that by telling this girl the truth about how she looks you're causing more damage than if you told a little white lie?"

"Can we get off this, please?" He sounded annoyed.

"Not until you agree that there are times when lying is justified."

"Of course not. Some people think when they're in a foreign country or dealing with women or on vacation that the usual standards don't apply."

"Like summer rules," I said.

"No such thing. There are no special situations when it comes to the truth."

"But . . ."

"I don't think you're ready to drive and carry

115

on a serious discussion," he said. "Make a choice."

"We can change the subject."

"Thank you. Michelle tells me you have a girl friend at camp."

"No big deal." I wanted to get off this, please.

"Who is she?"

"Just a girl."

"Does she have a name?"

"Sheila Bell."

He grunted. "Don't get mixed up with that Bell family. Some bunch they are."

"You were the one who made me go to Happy Valley. To get away from the Rumson family."

"Watch the road, please."

We finished the drive in silence, and barely talked through lunch. Then he went out on the lawn to read and doze in the hammock, and I went down to Marino's Beach to get out of his way. I didn't want to risk talking myself out of the driver's seat.

The Marinos didn't own the sandy beach and the boat dock and the snack bar anymore. A Greek family had bought them out and changed the name to Spiro's Lakeside. But I still called it

Marino's. That's how you could tell the new-comers from the old-timers among the summer people—anyone who called it Spiro's wasn't around two summers ago. Of course, the all-year-rounders called the place by its original name, Smith's Dock.

I swam out to the diving platform and did a couple of sloppy somersaults and one half-decent jacknife off the twenty-foot-high board before I stretched out in the sun. I thought about renting a canoe and paddling across the lake to Happy Valley to look for Sheila, but it would probably be a wasted trip. And get both of us in trouble. She was stuck with Harley for the weekend, and the way Rose had dragged her away from me last night it was clear that the Bell family wasn't going to let anybody keep Sheila from her sum-mer's duty.

I got bored lying in the sun and went over to the snack bar. There were always guys and girls my age hanging out there. But today they bored me, too. Some of them were going into town that night to see *Shane* and they invited me along. I'd only seen it four times.

I told them I had something better to do.

Think about Sheila.

Dinner was so boring I thought I'd jump out of my skin. Michelle blabbed nonstop. She had spent the day singing into a tape recorder at Jerry's house. The last version of "Getting to Know You" was so fab-u-lous she didn't recognize her own voice, she said.

"Jerry says I have definite professional potential."

"Who would pay money to hear you sing?" I asked.

Michelle raised her nose so she could look down it at me. "We'll soon find out. Jerry's made arrangements to offer three performances. Two of them free for the bungalow colony, and one with admission for the general public."

I was impressed. "Boy, he really is making a big deal out of a little camp play."

"He no longer envisions it as a camp play. In fact, rehearsals will be at night."

"At night?"

"To take it out of the camp atmosphere and make it more professional, more Broadway. After the cookout last night we spent three hours measuring the casino stage. Jerry's sending the

dimensions to a friend of his who's a set de-
signer.''

"The Bells go for all this?" I asked.

"Are you serious? It's good publicity, plus a
share of the profits plus free entertainment for
the bungalow colony.''

"Trust the Bells to turn a buck," said my
father.

"Speaking of the Bells," said Michelle, "Harley
turned the casino inside out last night. He swiped
the key to the storage closet where they keep the
dance records and put it in his mouth. He threat-
ened to swallow it if anyone came near him.''

She raised her eyebrows at me. "Finally, Rose
dragged in your little friend Sheila from God
knows where, and she got Harley to spit it
out.''

"Your little friend Sheila?" asked my mother.
"Someone we should know about?''

"Just another counselor." I shrugged casually.
Mom was fishing for information the way Dad
had in the car. "I sometimes ask her advice
about Harley.'' I was astonished at my cool.

"How's it going with Harley?" asked my
father.

"Terrible," I said. "He's a monster."

"Did you discuss him with Moe at your meeting?" asked Mom.

"Moe shot me right down."

"You ought to try to get him involved in some special activities," said my mother, "something that will absorb his energies, something with positive reinforcement."

"I'll try," I said, without much enthusiasm.

"It's a proven fact," said Mom, "that students are less disruptive when they feel they are part of the mainstream."

And then it hit me. It was brilliant. It was the best idea I'd had in sixteen years.

I couldn't wait for Monday morning.

13

There were tears in Moe Bell's eyes. "God bless you, Bobby Marks."

"It's nothing," I said humbly.

"You're some human being." He squeezed my shoulders.

"Well, I just had this feeling that inside Harley was a good boy struggling to get out, and I . . ."

But Moe was already striding away from me. By the time I caught up to him, he was in a corner of the casino stage, switching on the camp's public-address system.

"Attention please, attention please. This is Moe. Will Jerry Silver and Al Rapp please report to the casino immediately. That's Jerry and Al, to the casino, on the double."

I said, "I better get back to my group before..."

"I want you with me . . ."

". . . they tear up arts and crafts."

". . . when I tell them the news. I want you to get the credit you deserve."

I was afraid of that. "I'll take the cash and let the credit go."

He looked hurt. "That's not the Bobby Marks I know."

"It's from the *Rubaiyat* of Omar Khayyam," I admitted. Honors English.

He looked relieved. "You know, Bobby, I pride myself as a judge of young people. After twenty-two years in the school system, I should be. I knew from the moment I met you that you were a good person."

Moe patted my cheek. "Sometimes you give the impression of being a bit of a smart aleck. Maybe even a conniver. But that's just a cover. Inside you're all heart."

Before I could start feeling too sleazy, Al jogged into the casino. He was carrying a bat. Jerry was a step behind him.

"What is it, Moe? I'm right in the middle of tryouts for the softball team."

"Games," snorted Moe. "I want to talk about salvaging a human life."

"Oh, that," said Jerry. "I thought it was going to be something important."

"No jokes," snapped Moe. "And no discussion. Starting this minute, I want both of you to work Harley into your special programs."

"No can do," said Al.

"Two words," said Jerry. "Im-possible."

"You'll do it or I'll cancel the programs," said Moe.

"He's a problem child," said Al.

"There are no problem children, only weak teachers." Moe sounded very forceful. For the first time, I could believe that he was the assistant principal of a junior high school in the city.

"Well," I said, "better be getting back . . ."

Moe reached out and grabbed my sleeve. "As Bobby put it so well, Harley needs to be involved in absorbing activities with positive reinforcement. Al, I want Harley playing a starting position on the team. I don't want him stuck in the outfield where he'll get bored. Something in the mainstream. Bobby suggested shortstop."

"Shortstop," wailed Al. "That's a key position."

"Second base would be okay," I said, trying to be helpful.

Al looked as though he was going to break the bat. "What's the point of fielding a team if . . ."

"Winning isn't everything," said Moe. He turned to Jerry. "You'll find Harley a good role. Something with at least one big song and lots of time on stage."

"Why don't you just kill me, Moe?" Jerry opened his shirt. "Stab me here."

"Bobby," asked Moe, "what were your two suggestions?"

"Either Anna's son," I said, careful not to look at Jerry, "or Chulalongkorn, the Prince of Siam."

"The Prince," said Moe. "I like the Prince."

"Not the Prince," cried Jerry. "You are deliberately destroying my show."

"What's a show compared to a human life?" said Moe. "What's wrong with you two? You're not at camp to win games or put on shows, you're at camp to help children grow and learn, to give them happy and enriching summer experiences." He put his arm around me. "I'm glad Bobby understands what a camp is all about."

Al and Jerry looked at me with expressions of

pure hate. Killer glares. I told myself, Who cares what they think? But I still felt uncomfortable.

Moe released me. "Go get Harley. I want Al and Jerry to invite him personally. In front of me. So he really feels wanted."

I couldn't wait to tell Sheila. I sprinted toward arts and crafts, then circled the casino and snuck into the kitchen.

Sheila was at the counter, making sandwiches for lunch. I tiptoed up behind her. A wisp of black hair that had escaped the red bandanna was curled on the pale skin of the nape of her neck. I had an urge to kiss it, but I didn't have the nerve. I just touched it.

She whirled around, a knife in her hand. Her eyes widened. She started to smile, then frowned.

"You better get out of here," she whispered. "Rose said if she sees us together she'll have you fired."

"Don't sweat it."

"She really meant it, Bob. She doesn't want me to see you. She's afraid something will happen."

"Like what?"

"You know what."

"No, I don't." I really didn't.

Sheila looked down. "That, you know, I'll get . . ."

"That?" I pretended to be offended, but I was sort of flattered. Nobody had ever considered me a dangerous ladies' man before. "She really trusts you, doesn't she?"

"Rose doesn't trust anybody. If she so much as sees us talking together she'll go straight to Moe and he'll . . ."

"He'll tell her to mind her own business."

"You wish."

"Better believe it, Sheila. Yours truly has come up with a plan to set you free from Harley. At least some of the time."

She cocked her head to one side and peered at me out of the corner of one eye. Her lips were pressed together, the nostrils of her sharp little nose were flared, and her forehead was wrinkled. She looked adorable.

"What are you talking about, Bob?"

"Al is going to start Harley on the camp softball team and Jerry is going to give him a big role in the show. Harley's going to be spending most of his waking hours either practicing or rehearsing."

"You're living in a dreamworld. Al and Jerry would never do that."

"They have no choice. Moe loves the idea. He already told them they have to do it."

"I don't know." She shook her head. I thought she'd be jumping for joy, or at least flashing that dazzling smile that lit up her green eyes and flipped my heart like a pancake.

"And here's the best part. Rehearsals are at night, which means that you and I . . ."

"Think about Harley for a minute," she said. "He's a very sensitive little boy. You can't pass him around like a hot potato."

I switched gears. "Don't you think I planned this for Harley's sake? I spent the weekend discussing his case with a person who almost has a master's degree in educational psychology." I didn't think it was necessary to tell her that the person was my mother. "This person advised me that the best thing for Harley is to become involved in absorbing activities with positive reinforcement."

"Truly?"

"Harley needs to feel wanted. Useful. He has to start getting attention for the right reasons for a change. This could do it."

"You really think so?" She wanted to be convinced.

"It's worth a chance, isn't it?"

"But Jerry and Al? I wouldn't count on them to help anybody. Not those two. They're both so conceited."

"We'll keep tabs on the situation," I said. "It's not as if we're abandoning Harley. In fact, let's you and I take him to the casino tonight together. Jerry's holding the first auditions after supper."

"You'd do that?"

"Sure. And if things go well, if Harley seems calm and happy, we could take a little walk in the woods . . ."

She flashed the dazzling smile. Lights. Flip. I leaned forward and kissed her. "I've got to get Harley now. See you later."

I dashed out and flew to arts and crafts. I must have flown, because I don't remember my feet touching the ground.

14

Suddenly, camp was fun.

I woke up eager to get there, and I came home feeling terrific. With Harley away from the group, practicing softball for two hours in the morning and an hour in the afternoon, I was no longer a full-time human shock absorber. I was able to get to know the other kids. The first thing I did was change the group's name to the Rumson Rangers.

During one rest hour, I took Douglas for a private walk by the lake and described how fat I had been when I was his age. At first he didn't believe me. I told him that until I was fourteen years old, every pair of pants I wore was so tight it felt as though my guts were being squeezed up into my throat. Then he believed me. Only another fat boy could know what it was like to be strangled by your own pants. I demonstrated how in those days I was always pulling the seat of my pants out of the crack in my backside, just like he did now. We laughed together, and I thought Douglas stood a little straighter on the walk back to the casino.

I learned to tell Larry and Barry apart. And I realized what an enormous difference there was between them. Barry was the boss and Larry was his shadow. Whatever Barry did or said, Larry copied or repeated. For example, whenever we had juice for a snack, Barry would cover the top of the cup with the palm of his hand and shake it up before he drank it. Then he would look over at Larry to make sure his brother did exactly the same thing. Larry always did.

Little by little, I separated Barry and Larry. I assigned each of them a different buddy for swimming and I never allowed them to be on the same doubles team when we played handball. I gave Larry special responsibilities, like carrying the pocketknife when we went on nature hikes.

I worked on Miles' self-confidence. I taught him how to tread water and I helped him make a leather wallet for his father.

The only camper who didn't get the benefit of my new freedom from Harley was Steven. He seemed so healthy and well adjusted I decided to let him alone.

Harley was much calmer and quieter whenever he did join the group. My plan was working better than I'd ever imagined. Nobody had ever offered Harley a real chance to shine at anything before, and he seemed determined to prove how good he could be. Every day, Al hit hundreds of grounders to him at second base, and pitched extra batting practice to him. He was running Harley ragged, and Harley ate it up.

Sheila wasn't satisfied. She thought Al was "insincere," that he was giving Harley so much attention only because he didn't want Harley to be a drag on his precious team.

"So what?" I said. "As long as Harley thinks he's wanted he'll feel wanted. He'll act human. It could even get to be a habit."

"But it's all based on a lie," she said. "Al doesn't care about Harley. He just wants to be a big shot with a winning team."

"Illusion, not lies," I said. "In this play by

Pirandello called *Right You Are If You Think You Are . . ."*

"This is real life, not plays," she said.

Moe was ecstatic. Whenever he saw me, he winked or patted me on the back or said something nice like "There's the fella who put the happy back in Happy Valley." He never mentioned raising my salary back to the original $150, but I figured he was planning to surprise me with a whopping bonus. Anyway, who could think of money? What could be better than having a good time doing a worthwhile job?

And I was having a good time. After camp I'd go home on the bus, take a shower, shave whether I needed to or not, eat supper if my stomach wasn't fluttering too hard, and go back to Happy Valley with Michelle, in the car. She would go into the casino for rehearsal and I would wander over to the softball field and pretend to watch the evening pickup game.

As soon as I thought no one was watching me, I'd cut through the waist-high grass of the meadow above the field, run crouching along the tree line, double back twice just in case I was being followed, then work my way down to a quiet, mossy patch in a grove of trees I had discovered on a nature hike.

Within ten minutes, Sheila would appear.

We would have preferred to go back to the waterfront area, but it was too far from the casino if Harley threw a tantrum. Jerry had warned Sheila that at the first sign of trouble he would get on the P.A. and call her, but so far Harley was the best-behaved kid in the show. Even Michelle admitted it, although she said she thought it was only temporary. She expected Harley to blow up and ruin the show and her big chance for stardom. She said she'd never forgive me. Meanwhile, Jerry was working Harley as hard as Al was. Harley's singing voice wasn't particularly good, but it was loud. Jerry thought he could teach Harley to carry a tune well enough so that he wouldn't be an embarrassment to the show.

Sheila trusted Jerry about as much as she trusted Al.

"Between them," she said, "they'll drive that poor kid crazy."

"It'll be a short drive," I said. "Did we come here to discuss your cousin, or what?"

"Or what," she said, cuddling in my arms.

After an hour or so, we'd slip back to the casino by separate routes, although I didn't think we were fooling anybody, especially since we'd sit together in a dark corner of the casino sneaking kisses until the rehearsal ended.

One time, we didn't notice that Jerry was standing near us, listening for how well Michelle's voice carried to the back. He saw me stroke the front of Sheila's blouse. He looked away quickly, but I knew he saw it and I was glad.

I couldn't believe how fast two weeks whizzed by. I made the mistake of mentioning it to Sheila one evening while we were lying on our soft carpet of moss.

She sat up. "I know. The summer's almost over."

"C'mon, there are four more weeks of camp, then . . ."

"Before you turn around it'll be Labor Day."

I reached for her. "Well, we better make the most . . ."

She leaned away. "Are we going to see each other in the city?"

"Why not?"

"That's no answer," she said sharply.

I wasn't thrilled by her tone, so I said, "It's barely August, I don't think we have to talk about . . ."

"I think we do," she said. "If driving up to the Bronx is going to be too big a deal for you, I'd like to know now."

Driving. Even with my Junior License, which I hadn't taken the test for yet, I couldn't drive inside the city limits.

While I was picturing myself spending hours on the subway from Queens to the Bronx, Sheila said, in a softer tone, "Maybe I could come down and meet you at college sometimes."

College. I tried to remember if I had actually told Sheila that I was going to college in the fall. I was almost positive I hadn't lied about that. For all the hours we had spent together the last two weeks, we had done very little talking. And when we did talk, I was purposely hazy on certain topics, especially anything concerning age. If she found out I was only sixteen, she'd leave me in a cloud of dust. Since I was supposed to be eighteen years old, and most eighteen-year-olds had been graduated from high school, and since I was always quoting books and plays,

I figured she just naturally assumed I would be going to college in the fall. Since I hadn't mentioned going away to college, she must have assumed I would be going to a college in the city.

"Unless you don't want me to meet you at college," she said, starting to button her blouse.

"I didn't say that."

"You didn't say anything."

"I was thinking," I said.

"About what?"

"About how we're having our first fight. Over nothing."

"It's not nothing. If you're not sorry, I'm leaving."

"Sorry for what? You want me to take back something I didn't say?"

"You know, Bob, you have a real knack for twisting things around."

"Thanks a million. And you really know how to make a big deal out of nothing."

"You keep saying it's nothing. You think my coming here with you is nothing? I've let you go farther than any other boy."

Big deal, I thought. After two weeks she

finally let me reach inside her blouse to rub her brassiere, which felt like armor plate.

Then I felt glad. At least she hadn't let anybody else do what she didn't let me do. I had wondered if Sheila was a virgin, but I hadn't had the nerve to ask. What if she wasn't, and admitted it? What if she asked me if I was a virgin? I certainly didn't want to admit that I was.

"A penny for your thoughts," she said. I hated that expression.

"I was thinking about college," I said.

"What about college?"

I forced myself to think about college. "Basketball games. Fraternity parties . . ."

"Are you going to pledge a fraternity?" She leaned toward me.

"How should I know?"

"Would you let some girl wear your fraternity pin?"

I couldn't believe it. "Which girl?"

"Some girl you liked a lot?"

"If I thought she really liked me," I said, "I guess I'd let some girl wear my fraternity pin."

That must have answered Sheila's question because she let me pull her down to the carpet of moss, and a moment later she let me work my fingers inside her bra.

On the ride home that night, Michelle said, "Why so quiet? Sheila got your tongue?"

"Buzz off."

"Aren't we touchy tonight." Michelle was in one of her rare playful moods. "So how are you making out with the Brooklyn Bombshell?"

"She lives in the Bronx."

"Same difference. Jerry calls them all Borough Bagel Babies."

"What does he know about girls? He looks to me like he pees sitting down."

"Bobby!" She nearly drove off the road. "That's the most disgusting thing I ever heard."

"Maybe you want to tell me how you're making out with him."

"Not that you would understand," she said in her snottiest voice, "but Jerry and I have a platonic relationship. Our minds and our souls are artistically one. We don't need to roll around on the ground."

"What does that mean?"

"Tell me why you and Sheila never bother brushing off your clothes when you're done. Are you trying to prove something? Do you think other people actually care what you're doing?''

''At least we do what real men and women do.''

''You don't say.'' She curled her lip. ''Tell me, hot pants, has she asked you yet if you'll see her in the city? Has she started angling for some little token of your esteem, say a slave bracelet or a fraternity pin?''

''You think you know everything.''

''You're so naive, Bobby. A sixteen-year-old girl is a woman and a sixteen-year-old boy is a child.''

We didn't say another word the rest of the way home. In the driveway, before she even turned off the engine, I jumped out of the car and ran into the house. Mom looked up from a book as I whipped through the living room.

''Is anything . . .'' she said, but I just waved good night and kept traveling. I snatched two peaches out of the refrigerator and headed for my room.

''Don't forget to wash them,'' called my mother. How does everyone know my business? I thought. To spite her, I ran the water in the kitchen sink for a few seconds without getting the peaches wet.

I slammed my door. In bed, listening to Eddie Fisher singing "I'm Walking Behind You" and dribbling peach juice over my chest, I felt better. Michelle was just jealous.

Sheila was a nice girl, she didn't put out for everybody. She wanted some assurance that I wasn't just after her body, that I cared about her as a person. She had a right to know if this was just a summer fling for me. Of course, that didn't mean I had to tell her the truth.

Whatever that was.

Thinking about Sheila, I felt again the throbbing heat that took over me when I lay close to her on our mossy carpet. I closed my eyes and stroked myself as that good, exciting feeling filled my body to bursting.

Later, drifting toward sleep, I wondered if Michelle might know something I didn't know.

15

Willie Rumson showed up at Happy Valley in the beginning of the sixth week of camp. He was sitting loose as a rag doll on the back of a tractor that Jim Smith was driving. A cold stone I hadn't felt in two years settled to the bottom of my stomach.

I knew this summer was too good to be true.

I was goofing off on the casino steps with some other counselors, waiting for the end of rest hour, when the tractor pulled up in a storm of loose dirt. Jim waved me over.

"That punk a friend of yours?" asked Al.

"Jimbo's okay," I said. I sauntered down the steps and over to the tractor. I hooked my thumbs in my belt and hunched my shoulders forward. I don't know who I was trying to impress the most

141

with my cool, the counselors or Jim and Willie or myself.

"Long time no see," I said to Jim.

"How you been?" Jim leaned down from the tractor seat to shake my hand. "Say hello to Willie. Make him feel good."

"How they hanging, Willie?"

He bobbed his head. "Real good, real good."

The pointed rat face I remembered was now a dopey moon. Willie Rumson's eyes were glazed. His fat cheeks were smooth as a baby's. That blond hair he used to wear in a greasy duck's ass was chopped down to a crew cut. His body, once lean and wiry, looked swollen and soft. Jim was right, Willie did look like a zombie now. The only thing that hadn't changed was the Marine Corps insignia tattooed on his left arm over the word "Willie."

"You remember Bob Marks?" asked Jim.

"Sure, sure, sure." Spittle formed in the corners of his mouth. "Old buddy, Bob Marks."

It was hard to believe this was the same Willie Rumson who had haunted my fourteenth summer, who had ridiculed me for being fat, chased me and beat me and stripped me and nearly killed me.

"Hey, Willie," said Jim. "You and Bob had some times together, you remember?"

"Some times." Willie's grin widened to show stretches of toothless gum. "Me and Bob."

Some times. I almost felt sorry for him.

Jim lowered his voice. "You get the picture? Those shock treatments really screwed him up."

"Is he always like this?"

"This is one of his good days. Usually he just sits around the house, eating and drinking and watching television. One time he was up all night looking at test patterns."

"Can't they do anything for him?"

"They done too much already. Listen, Marks, can you help me out?"

"How?"

"I'm gonna be working around here most of the week. I'm gonna try to keep Willie with me, get him some fresh air, you know? He might wander around a little, but he won't bother nobody. Could you sort of keep an eye out so he don't hurt himself? And tell your friends?" He nodded toward the counselors who were standing on the steps, trying to eavesdrop on our conversation.

"Sure, Jim. You can count on it." I was glad to do him a favor. I knew it had to be important for him to ask.

He gave me a warm smile. "Thanks, Marks. I always figured you weren't like most of the summer people." He nodded toward the casino steps. "Some good-lookers over there. You getting your nookie this summer?"

"I'm doing all right. Want to meet any of them?"

He shook his head. "Them days are over. I'm getting married after Labor Day when the trailer's ready."

"Married?"

"Have to." He shrugged. "Would of married her anyway, she's a real nice girl." He shook my hand again. "I really appreciate this, Marks. Willie needs to get out of the house but I can't watch him every minute."

He gunned the engine. As the tractor pulled away, Willie gave me a big, sweet, silly smile and waved, just like a little kid. As bad as he had been, there was something pathetic about the way he was now.

The counselors crowded around me. Al asked, "Wasn't that the Rummie who burned old Dr. Kahn's place?"

"Yeah, but he's harmless now," I said.

"Who told you that? The other Rummie?"

I ignored Al. "Willie might be wandering around the area this week. If he looks like he might hurt himself, I'd appreciate it if you'd call me or Jim Smith, that's the guy driving the tractor."

"We need a crazy punk around here like we need a dog with rabies," said Al. "We got all these kids to worry about."

"I don't think he'd hurt a fly," I said.

"We can't take a chance," said Al. "I don't want him around."

"Who cares what you want?" I snapped.

Al took off his glasses and squinted at me. "You're going to open your mouth one time and find a fist in it."

Sheila appeared on the casino steps, her curly hair damp and her cheeks flushed from cleaning the kitchen after lunch. I wasn't going to back down from anybody in front of her.

"You think beating me up is going to make you taller?"

There was a shocked silence, then Moe's voice boomed over the P.A. "Rest Hour is over. Counselors pick up your groups."

Saved by a Bell, I thought.

The counselors repeated my line to each other as they headed back into the casino. Al hadn't moved. His ears had turned pink.

"You cocky bastard," he said, "someday you're going to get your head handed to you."

"But not today," I Bogied. I walked past him, winked at Sheila, and swaggered into the casino. In a moment, I knew, I'd be trembling all over, but right now I felt like Shane.

16

We were rolling around on the ground when Sheila abruptly broke free and sat up. "We never talk," she said.

"Our mouths have better things to do," I said.

"That's all you ever want to do. Is that all I mean to you?"

I sat up. In the darkness, I couldn't make out her expression, but I could imagine it. Her lips were pressed together, the nostrils of her sharp little nose were flared and her forehead was wrinkled. Her head was cocked to one side and she was peering at me out of the corner of one eye, although if I couldn't see her how could she see me? The first hundred times or so I thought it was an adorable expression, but now I was beginning to wish she'd try on something else for a change. Even when I couldn't see it.

"I asked you a question, Bob. Is that all I mean to you?"

I had an answer on the tip of my tongue, an old schoolyard line I had copied in my notebook. *I don't love you for sex alone, baby, it's your body, too*. It was a funny line but Sheila had no sense of humor. She thought *Mad Comics* was sick.

"What do you want to talk about?" I asked.

"Anything you want to talk about." She seemed satisfied even though I hadn't answered her question.

I thought of topics. She hated western movies so we couldn't discuss the hidden meanings in *Shane*. She wasn't much of a reader. She knew a lot of gossip about pop singers and movie stars but that didn't interest me. I knew she'd like to know more about Willie Rumson and why I stuck up for him, but I was afraid that could lead to a discussion of what happened two years ago which might give her clues to my real age. I still wasn't sure exactly how old she was, although I knew she only had a semester left of high school.

Finally, I said, "A really interesting thing happened at lunch today."

"What was that, dear?" She said it just like a wife on one of those dumb television comedies.

"Remember I told you about the Stern twins? How Larry copies Barry? Well, today at lunch, Barry put his hand over his juice cup, just like he always does, shook it up, and looked at Larry to make sure he was doing the same thing.

"Well, Larry just drank his juice down without shaking it. And when Barry said, 'You forgot to shake your juice,' Larry said, 'I do it my own way now.' And he stood up and started hopping up and down. You get it? To shake up the juice."

"Of course I get it," said Sheila. "Did you tell him it was a stupid way to shake up the juice? That he could give himself a terrible stomachache?"

"That's not the point, Sheila. Larry is starting to think for himself."

"What's the good of thinking for yourself if you act like a moron?"

"Don't you understand, Larry was completely dominated by his sibling and now . . ."

"You'd make a great psychiatrist," she said. I could tell from her voice she was serious.

"Not me. That means taking chemistry and physics in college and going to medical school . . ."

"What's wrong with going to medical school?"

"I don't want to be a doctor. I want to be a writer."

"Doctors have better lives," said Sheila.

"Says who?"

"People look up to doctors, they make more money than . . ."

"Ernest Hemingway's doing just fine, thank you."

"Is he the one with the beard?"

What could I say? Obscenity? I thought, What am I doing here? How could I spend the summer with a girl who barely knows who Hemingway is? How could I even think about seeing her in the winter in the city?

After a while, I said, "Yeah, he's the one with the beard." I felt tired, and for the first time I wished that Jerry would call for Sheila on the P.A.

"A penny for your thoughts."

"Make it ten cents," I said, quick and nasty.

"That's what Harley owes me from the first day I ever saw him."

"I'm glad you brought that up. Have you looked at Harley lately? I mean closely? He's got circles under his eyes and he's losing weight."

"He's been acting like a normal kid for a change," I said.

"But that's not normal for him. I think Al and Jerry are pushing him too hard."

"I'll check into it," I said.

"Thank you." She put her arms around my neck. "See? We can have an intelligent discussion."

The next day, while the Rumson Rangers were at arts and crafts, I nonchalantly drifted over to the softball field. Al saw me but he didn't even nod.

Harley was staggering around second base like a drunk. His tongue was hanging out and his white tee-shirt was gray with sweat. He was stopping most of the grounders that Al was hitting to him, but some of the line drives were

151

knocking him down. He was the smallest and the youngest boy on the field.

I waited until Al organized batting practice, then I joined him behind the backstop. "If you don't mind, I'd like to take Harley to free swim with the group now."

"I mind." He pulled the visor of his baseball cap down over his horn-rimmed glasses. Harley was the first batter. Al shouted, "Dig in, you're standing like a girl. You afraid of the ball?"

"I think he could use a little break," I said.

"I think he could use more practice."

"The kid looks bushed, Al, he needs a . . ."

"Look here. You stuck me with the brat. Okay, I'm going to win with him." He crossed his arms and puffed up his chest. "I've got nothing more to say to you."

On the way back to arts and crafts, I stopped off at the kitchen. Sheila poured me a cup of cold grapefruit juice.

"Al's ticked off at me. He won't listen. Do you think I should say something to Moe?"

"Moe wants him on the team. So does Rose. And Irving's tickled pink. He stays in the city and he gets good reports. Nobody tells him that Harley moans all night."

"He moans?"

"His legs hurt him from playing so much baseball. You should see the blisters on his feet. And after he does fall asleep, he talks."

"About what?"

"Lines from the show. He's so scared he's going to forget his lines."

"We really ought to do something," I said.

Sheila patted my cheek. "You'll think of something. My psychiatrist."

I left her, feeling trapped.

At dinner that evening I casually mentioned that Harley was looking dead tired. I would have gone into more detail if I had been alone with my mother. I might even have told her about the incident with Al and what Sheila had told me about Harley moaning at night. But Michelle was there and I didn't trust her.

Mom said, "Maybe it's too much pressure on Harley, playing on the team and also being in the show. If you think that's the case, maybe you could help him choose between the two."

Some choice, I thought. If he quit the team,

he'd be back with the group, making my days miserable. If he quit the play, I'd lose my nights with Sheila. And I wasn't ready to give up those nights yet. Who knows, we might make it to the Island yet.

"Tell him to drop the play," said Michelle. "There's another boy who would be so much better as the Prince."

"I'm disappointed in you, Michelle," said Mom. "I'm sure Bobby agrees that the choice should be made with Harley's best interest in mind."

Michelle looked sheepish and I felt like a complete hypocrite. No wonder I didn't trust Michelle. Who could trust me?

Sheila was surprised to see me waiting for her outside the casino that night. As soon as Harley trudged in for rehearsal, she whispered, "Why aren't you up at our place?"

"I thought you were worried about Harley."

"I am. So what?"

"So I thought we better see what's going on here."

"You sure that's the reason?" She gave me

her formerly adorable expression. Why did it get on my nerves now?

The rehearsal was more interesting than I thought it would be. I got to hear Michelle sing "Hello, Young Lovers" with a musical accompaniment. She was good! Her voice was strong and sweet, her movements were graceful, she looked beautiful on stage. Maybe she did have professional potential. My sister, the star!

I was so absorbed in her performance that I didn't realize that Sheila had slipped her hand into mine until she said, "It's like that song was written for us."

"There are people around."

"That never bothered you before."

Harley walked out onstage blinking his eyes a mile a minute and nervously wiping his palms on his pants. When Jerry started yelling directions at him, Harley grabbed his elbows and hugged himself, as if he was cold.

They were rehearsing a scene at the end of the play. The King had just died and Anna had decided to stay in Siam and help the young Prince become a better king than his father. Jerry was demonstrating to Harley how to walk and hold his head and move his arms so that the audience would understand that he was growing up fast and assuming some of the forceful mannerisms of his dead father. Yet not so fast that there wasn't still a lot of the little boy left in him.

I had trouble following it all. It was just too complicated for a ten-year-old who had never been in a play before. The harder Harley tried to follow Jerry's directions, the worse he acted and the more Jerry rolled his eyes and slapped his forehead and threw up his hands. Jerry was trying to impersonate the director of a Broadway show as surely as Al was making believe he was a big-league manager. No wonder Harley was moaning at night.

Michelle put her arm around Harley and whispered to him until his body relaxed. They rehearsed the scene a few more times, and although Harley improved, Jerry made it clear by his gestures that it still wasn't good enough for him.

When the rehearsal was over, I walked out of the casino so deep in thought that I forgot about Sheila. I went straight to our car.

"I have time for a short walk." Sheila's voice startled me.

"Uh . . . Michelle's going to be right out. I don't want to miss my ride home."

"You never used to worry about that. You never used to mind walking home."

"I'm really tired tonight, Sheila."

"Maybe you're just tired of me." When I didn't answer right away, she said, "Is bored a better word, Mr. Writer?"

"We can miss a night, Sheila." I was annoyed by her needling tone. "Since we do the same thing all the time."

"You can say anything you want, but I'm not going all the way with you. Not this summer."

"What does that mean, not this summer?"

"Just what I said."

"Does it mean you'll do it this winter? Or next summer?"

"Bob, I don't like it when you talk to me like that."

"Like what?"

"Hello, young lovers," said Michelle in her most sarcastic tone.

Sheila rushed away and I got into the car.

157

Michelle must have felt guilty, because she said, "I'll wait if you want to kiss and make up."

"Just drive," I said.

"Just drive," she mimicked.

Michelle was quiet on the way home, which was too bad for once. I wanted to talk to her but I didn't know how to start the conversation without sounding like I needed advice, which I did. Harley looked as though he was heading for a nervous breakdown, and it was partly my fault. Sheila and I were heading for a nervous breakup. And here I was, still being driven around by my sister. Bobby Marks Rides Again! When was I going to be in the driver's seat? Of my own life?

I went to sleep trying to figure out what I should do, and I woke up without any new brainstorms. I was so preoccupied the next morning that I didn't notice Willie Rumson sitting on the casino steps until opening ceremonies were over. He was on the top step, grinning and nodding at campers streaming past him toward their first activities of the day. He was drinking from a beer bottle and flicking a cigarette lighter on and off. I didn't see Jim but I heard his tractor up in the meadow.

Al swaggered up. "Beat it, you punk," he bellowed at Willie.

Before anyone could move, Al charged up the casino steps. He grabbed the front of Willie's shirt and his belt, and heaved him off the steps.

Willie hit the ground with a sickening *thunk*, but he got right up, a puzzled expression on his face. I ran over to him.

"Why'd he do that?" whined Willie.

I had no answer for him. I brushed off his shirt.

Moe pushed through the crowd of campers and counselors forming around us. "Is he all right?" When I nodded, Moe turned to Al and asked, "Was that necessary?"

"Just look at that ex-con firebug, getting drunk and waving his lighter around." Al's face was flushed. "You want him to do the same thing to that firetrap of a casino he did to Dr. Kahn's house?"

"Toolshed," I corrected.

Moe blew his whistle. "Counselors, move these kids out to their first activities, let's go."

Douglas brought me Willie's bottle, which hadn't broken, and his lighter, a silver Zippo with a Marine Corps insignia on one side. I gave them to Willie. He pressed the bottle and the lighter against his chest like a little kid hugging his toys.

I turned Willie around and pointed him toward the meadow. "Now you go to Jim—he's expecting you."

"Sure, sure, sure." He shuffled off without a backward look.

"Just gonna let him go, huh?" said Al.

"He hasn't done anything," I said.

"That's true," said Moe. But his eyes flicked back and forth between Al and me.

"Keep your fingers crossed," said Al, walking away. "He hasn't done anything *yet*."

I dragged Harley out of the casino during rest hour. He said he wanted to take a nap, but I told him it was important that we talk. He rubbed his eyes as we walked along the tree line toward the top of the meadow. The high grass that Jim Smith had mowed was turning yellow and dry in the sun. It crinkled under our feet and spewed up dust that tickled our noses.

"What's so important we have to come up here? It stinks up here."

Maybe it was only my imagination, but Harley's

red hair and his blue eyes, both so bright at the beginning of camp, seemed paler and duller now. The sharp nastiness in his voice was gone, too, replaced by a cranky whine.

"I think I know why you're so tired, Harley. You're the only kid in camp with a big part in the show and a starting position on the team."

"So?"

"It's too much for one person."

"I can do it."

"But you're knocking yourself out. You could have more fun if you concentrated on just one."

"I can't quit." He looked grim. He was really determined not to let those creeps down. Or himself.

"You don't have to quit. If you decide to play second base you could be a member of the Siamese children's chorus instead of the Prince. And if you decide to be the Prince, you could play outfield instead of second base. What do you say?"

"It's too late. The tournament starts next week. The show's next week, too."

"It's not too late. I'll talk to Al and Jerry for you. Just say the word."

"Let's go back." He spun around and started walking quickly back to the casino. I thought the discussion was over, but halfway back, he whirled to face me. "Which one?"

Did I want my days or my nights? The Rumson Rangers or Sheila?

"You have to choose, Harley. Whichever is more important to you."

He shook his head and turned away. I followed his gaze. Below us, the softball field and the casino rippled behind waves of midday heat.

"I wish one of them would disappear," he said. "Then I wouldn't have to choose."

"It'll be all right, whichever you choose."

"Says who?"

"Believe me, Harley, Al and Jerry will understand."

"Believe you? Like with the buzzards on the roof?"

"That was different, Harley, that was . . ."

But he was already running away from me, down the slope toward the casino.

Believe me? Why should he?

Sheila was waiting for me on the steps of the casino.

"I'm sorry," she said. "Will you accept my apology, Bob? I was wrong."

My head was still filled with Harley. "What are you talking about?"

"Please don't make this harder for me. I was wrong and you were right last night." She clasped and unclasped her hands. "I thought you wouldn't respect me if I . . . you know."

"C'mon, Sheila, this is 1954."

"More in 'fifty-four," she said with a little laugh. When I didn't even smile, the laugh became a catch in her throat. "I thought you'd like that. You think I have no sense of humor."

"I never said that."

"You thought it." Bright red spots burned through her pale cheeks. "You think I'm not smart enough for you. I can tell. You know, reading isn't everything."

"I know that."

"You're just saying that. You'll say anything to get your way. Or if you think it's witty." She took a deep breath. "But when it comes to real feelings, you hide behind a book."

I silently prayed for Moe to rescue me again by announcing that rest hour was over.

Sheila said, "I don't even know how you really feel about me."

"I'm only with you every night."

"You never said you loved me."

"I never said that to any girl."

"Am I just any girl?"

When I didn't answer right away, she asked, "Will I see you tonight?"

Her face twisted into that ex-adorable expression.

"Why not?" I said.

I walked into the casino so I wouldn't have to look at her.

17

When Michelle and I got home from camp that afternoon there was a brand-new Cadillac in the driveway. Mom was waiting for us in the doorway, smiling happily. She smelled of strong perfume.

"Surprise!" she said as she stepped aside.

The Millers were in the living room. Photographs and picture postcards and travel brochures from their European vacation were spread over the coffee table. Joanie jumped up when we walked in. She looked very sophisticated, and older. She wore a ton of makeup and her hair was cut short.

She hugged Michelle and gave me a kiss on each cheek. "It's very continental," she explained.

I felt strange so I made a joke. "I guess I should sing La Mayonnaise."

Mr. Miller guffawed. "Better work on your pronunciation, Ro-bair. The French national anthem is 'La Marseillaise.'"

"Bob knows that," said Joanie. "La Mayonnaise is for the French dressing."

Good old Joanie, she still appreciated a bad pun. We laughed together and I felt better than I had in days. I even forgot about Harley and Sheila for a while.

The Millers stayed for dinner. I was glad Dad was in the city so he didn't have to listen to Mr. Miller boast about how much money he was making. Two years ago, Mr. Miller had offered Dad a partnership in his new business, but Dad preferred security so he'd stayed with the company he had worked for since college. In two years, Mr. Miller made a fortune. So he claimed. It was probably true. He'd certainly spent a lot on our presents. The Millers had brought French perfume for Mom and a flowered red scarf for Michelle and an Italian leather belt for me. They even had a gift for Dad, a fancy silk tie, but Mr. Miller spoiled it by saying, "Don't let him wear it to that dump he works at."

During dinner, Joanie and Mrs. Miller described the museums and the cathedrals and the ruins they had visited. During dessert, Michelle said she had to get back to camp to rehearse. The Millers were insulted, but Michelle didn't care. Her mind was already on the stage. She glanced at me. "Going back?"

I shook my head.

She raised one eyebrow at a time, a trick Jerry had taught her. "Isn't someone expecting you?"

"I'm staying," I said.

Michelle winked. "Good for you."

After dinner, Mr. Miller stretched out on the couch while Mom and Mrs. Miller cleared the table. They excused Joanie and me so they could talk privately, and we went outside. I brushed off the chaise longue for Joanie and took the old wicker chair for myself. It was a mild evening, and already dark. The days were getting shorter. I could barely make out Joanie's face.

"How's your novel going?" she asked.

"My novel?"

"Wasn't this the summer you were going to have enough adventures to write a novel? That's what you said the last day of school."

"I was going to make a lot of notes." I

showed her all the empty pages in my notebook. "But I've been too busy. It's all up here." I tapped my head. "Did you know that Willie Rumson's back?"

"Ugh."

"His mind's gone. He was . . ."

"Bob." She leaned toward me. "I've got to tell you something." Her voice dropped to a whisper. "I'm in love."

"You sure it isn't heartburn? My mother's meat loaf . . ."

"Don't make a joke of this, Bob. It's the real thing. It happened in Paris."

I felt a stab of jealousy. But why? Joanie and I had never been anything but best friends. "Tell me about it."

"One morning I went to the Louvre. By myself. Daddy had to check for mail at American Express and Mom went with him. We arranged to rendezvous in front of the Mona Lisa."

The way she spoke, slowly, with dramatic pauses, I knew she had rehearsed the story. Or already told it a dozen times.

"I arrived early and I was standing in front of the painting, thinking, 'It's so much smaller than

I expected,' when a voice behind me said, 'I know what you're thinking. It's so much smaller than you expected.'

"I whirled around and suddenly I was gazing into the biggest, deepest, brownest eyes I had ever seen. I said, 'Who are you?' and he said . . .''

Joanie grabbed my wrist. "Listen to this, Bob. He said, 'I'm Nobody! Who are you? Are you nobody, too?'

"And I said, 'Then there's a pair of us—don't tell!' And he said . . .''

I couldn't contain myself. "He said, 'They'd banish us, you know.'''

"Who told you? My mother?" Joanie's voice was angry.

"Are you kidding? We did that poem last year in Honors English. Emily Dickinson, the second series.''

"I knew you'd appreciate my story," said Joanie. "And you'd like Stewart a lot.''

"Stewart?''

"Stewart Cowan. He's going into his junior year at Princeton.''

"And you fell in love at first sight over a couple of lines of a two-stanza poem?''

"We spent every day together for the next week. Stewart was bumming around Europe for the summer with his roommate. He changed his plans to meet us in London. Daddy was furious when he showed up."

"Your father never was big on Emily Dickinson," I said sarcastically.

"He's crazy about Stewart now. Stewart's so smart. He's a pre-med, but he takes as many literature courses as he can. He says he doesn't want to be one of those uncultured doctors. His favorite poet is William Butler Yeats. He's read *War and Peace* twice. When Mom asked him what he thought of it, he said, 'Loved war, hated peace.'"

"That's such an old joke," I said.

"If I didn't know you better, I'd think you sounded jealous." She squeezed my wrist. "We'll double-date in the city. Stewart and I and you and your new girl friend."

"What new girl friend?"

"C'mon, your mother told us you're really going hot and heavy with a girl from camp. What's she like?"

"Well, she's got green eyes and curly black

hair and she's really built." I sensed Joanie nodding as I talked. But I wasn't answering her question. I was telling her what Sheila looked like, not what she was like.

I didn't know what she was like.

"Hey, Princess, let's go," boomed Mr. Miller. "We've got to get up early."

Joanie stood up. "We're going back to the city tomorrow. Mom and I've got to shop for clothes. We're all going to Stewart's parents' house for dinner next week."

"You pinned yet?"

"Pardon me?"

"Nothing, just a private joke."

"I'm really glad we had a chance to talk. I wanted to share it with somebody who would understand."

After the Millers left, I climbed into the old backyard swing and pumped into the darkness. Far below me, fires glowed along the shore of Rumson Lake. Sure, I was jealous. Joanie and Stewart could talk poetry and make literary jokes with each other. Joanie appreciated Stewart's smart-aleck side. Sheila didn't know who I was any more than I knew who she was.

18

Harley seemed to be more relaxed the next morning. Had he made a decision?

I watched him on the softball field. He muffed a grounder and didn't even twitch when Al chewed him out. Had Harley decided to give up second base? That meant he'd be spending more time with the group. And Sheila would still be free at night while he rehearsed.

Was that what I wanted?

Why was I waiting for a ten-year-old to make a decision for me? If I wanted to stop seeing Sheila, why didn't I just tell her? Like a man.

I thought I'd talk to Harley at lunch and find out what was going on in his head, but I never got the chance. Sheila marched right up to my table while I was eating with the Rumson Rangers.

It was the first time I had ever seen her out of the kitchen during lunch, her busiest time of the day.

"Bob? Do you have to go home for dinner tonight?"

"Huh?"

"We'll have a picnic by the lake. Just the two of us. I'll make it. You'll like it, you really will. I promise. Okay?" Her green eyes were softer than I remembered them. Wavery. Pleading.

"Okay."

As she walked back to the kitchen, Barry started chanting, "Bob's got a girl friend, Bob's got a girl friend," until Larry said, "Why don't you just dry up and blow away." Barry looked flabbergasted.

If I had been in love with Sheila the way Joanie said she was in love with Stewart Cowan, that picnic by the lake would have been the most romantic moment of my life.

It was a perfect August evening, not a cloud in the soft blue sky, not a mosquito in the calm, warm air. The only sounds were the gentle slap of Rumson Lake against the camp rowboat, and the creak of the boat straining against its chain.

Sheila spread a white tablecloth on the grass. She set two places with white cloth napkins and real plates and stainless steel knives, forks, and spoons. She filled two glasses with iced tea from a thermos. She piled my plate with cold chicken, sliced tomato, potato salad, and little seeded rolls. She set out a bowl of large, ripe strawberries and covered them with cream.

I was hungry and the food was delicious. I was almost finished before I looked to see Sheila staring at me dreamily. She hadn't touched her own food.

"I love to watch you eat," she said.

We had eaten together only once before, I remembered. A month ago at the counselors' cookout on this very spot. She had done the eating for both of us. That time, I had been the one without an appetite.

"It's really delicious," I said.

"I love to cook," she said, "for someone special."

The food lost some of its taste. The warm air was stifling.

"How'd you manage to arrange all this?"

"Where there's a will there's a way." She

174

blew me a kiss. "I made up a story for Rose. She's going to give Harley dinner and make sure he gets to the casino on time for rehearsal. By the way, there's more chicken."

"Not right now, thanks."

"Last night, when you didn't come, I thought I'd never see you again. I cried all night."

I drank half a glass of iced tea, but the dryness in my throat returned immediately.

"I love you, Bob."

Now was the time to be honest with Sheila. To tell her the truth, that I didn't love her, that I didn't want to date her after the summer was over. If I didn't have the guts to say that, I could tell her I was only sixteen years old going into my senior year in high school. Then she would ditch me.

"I don't want to lose you, Bob."

I didn't have the guts to say anything. I told myself that Sheila had worked so hard on this picnic, it wouldn't be fair to spoil it. An alibi.

She started packing everything back into the wooden picnic basket. "We'll save it for later, when we come back."

"From where?"

"The island," she said.

I felt as though I was in a trance, that I was being controlled by some force outside my body. I helped her finish packing. We shook out the tablecloth and folded it into the basket.

She kissed me and took out a small key. She unlocked the chain that tied the rowboat to the trunk of a tree on the edge of the shore. I imagined the chain winding around my body, tying me to Sheila forever.

She screamed.

I rushed over and followed her trembling finger. On the otherside of the tree, in a tangle of high grass, lay a body. It was Willie Rumson.

"Is he . . ."

"Dead drunk," I said. I held up a nearly empty pint bottle of gin. Willie snored and smiled. He didn't open his eyes.

"He was there the whole time?"

"Don't worry, he didn't hear or see a thing. He's been out of it for a long time."

"Come on," she said. "Before he wakes up."

"Maybe I should do something for him."

"When we come back," she said.

176

She took my hand and led me to the boat. I helped her in and climbed in after her. We each lifted an oar to push off.

"Sheila? You sure about this?"

"It's what you want, isn't it? I want to prove that I really care about you."

"Maybe we should . . ."

She thrust the blade of the oar into the shallow water and pushed. The boat jerked away from the shore and I sat down hard. We drifted toward Make-Out Island.

"Are you all right, Bob? You look so pale."

My body was cold and my mind feverish. Could I be scared? Wasn't this exactly what I wanted, to get to Make-Out Island this summer, with Sheila?

But I'm not ready yet, I haven't thought about it enough. I'm not even carrying protection. I'm scared.

"Shall I row?" she asked.

"I'll row." We fitted the oars into the oarlocks. I pulled. The rowboat moved smoothly over the water. My knees were shaking so hard that my feet tap-danced on the bottom of the boat.

Sheila sat in the back of the boat, her hands folded in her lap. She was smiling at me. I thought it was a smug smile. Then I saw the knuckles of her hands. They were bone white. She was scared, too.

So why are we doing this? She doesn't really want to do it, she just thinks it's the only way to hold on to me.

She's right. If we do it, how will I be able to stop seeing her? You can't just ditch a girl after you do it, especially if it's the first time for both of you. She'll really have her hooks into me then, I thought.

I glanced over my shoulder. We were almost there. The trees of the island loomed over us. The island was so much closer than it had seemed to be when I'd thought I'd never get there.

Turn around. Go back. You're holding the oars. Don't do anything you don't want to do.

What's wrong with you? Maybe Jerry knew something when he put his hand on your knee. Most people would say that any guy who wouldn't jump at the chance to go to Make-Out Island with a piece like Sheila is some kind of a queer.

She had hardly moved since I had begun to row. The smile was frozen on her face. Her hands were locked together. Her eyes stared at me, as fixed as headlights. I heard her breathe in short, shallow gasps.

I couldn't look at her. I glanced over my shoulder again as the boat scraped over rocks in shallow water, then bumped up to the shore. I stood and slipped an oar out of the lock. I was about to pole us onto the island when I saw the fire.

On the mainland, up the Happy Valley hill, flames leaped out of the treetops and licked at the navy blue sky.

19

We gasped at the stink of wet, burned wood.
Firemen in black rubber coats swarmed over the
smoking, steaming hulk of the casino, shouting
over the crackle of their walkie-talkies. They
swung axes and sledgehammers and they dragged
thick, writhing hoses through the eerie patches of
light cast by the red blinkers and the spotlights
mounted on their fire trucks.

Sheila pulled at the sleeve of a fireman hurrying past. "Was anybody hurt?"

"Check First Aid." He pointed his hooked
pole toward arts and crafts.

The Rumson Lake Volunteer Fire Department
and Rescue Corps had set up a four-cot medical
tent behind the arts and crafts shack. The only
patient was Jerry Silver, who was reclining on

one of the cots while a man in a white jacket wrapped a yard of gauze around his left hand. Jerry looked happy. Michelle and the cast of *The King and I* were crowded into the tent with him. They were standing in their positions for the deathbed scene at the end of the show.

Jerry waved his right hand when he saw us. "Brother Roberto. And Sheila, Our Lady of the Lunches. Welcome."

"What happened?" I asked.

"'Tis nothing," said Jerry. He tossed his lion's-mane hair.

There were tears in Michelle's voice. "He went back in there to make sure all the kids were out."

"Where's Harley?" asked Sheila.

Jerry sat up. "Isn't he with you? He left rehearsal early to meet you, he said . . ."

Sheila bolted.

I ran after her. "Wait up."

"He's in there," she screamed over her shoulder. "It's my fault. I never should have gone with you."

"It's not your fault." I grabbed her.

"What do you know?" She struggled in my

181

arms. "You've got only one thing on your mind, that's all you care about. . ."

"No civilians allowed in this area." A fireman blocked our way. The word LIEUTENANT was engraved on the shield of his hat.

"There's a little boy in there," sobbed Sheila.

"Structure's clear, we've swept it twice," said the Lieutenant. "Now I told you folks to . . ."

"Lieutenant!" A fireman rushed up. He held something in his asbestos glove. "Look at this."

The Lieutenant stepped forward to meet him. "Oh, my God."

"I found it near the kitchen steps. Next to some rags and an empty kerosene can." The fireman's voice cracked. "I hate to be the one to tell Chief Rumson."

"I'll take care of it," said the Lieutenant.

Just before his hand closed over it, I saw Willie Rumson's silver Marine Corps lighter.

The two men hurried off.

"You know what that was?" I said to Sheila. "Willie's lighter. We better tell somebody we saw Willie down by the lake, dead drunk, before they try to pin the fire on him."

"Wait a minute." She grabbed my shirt. "You'll

have to tell them I was down there with you, that we rowed to Make-Out Island . . .''

''So what?''

''That's great for you, but what about me? What kind of reputation do you think I'll get?''

''C'mon, Sheila, this is serious.''

''They won't do anything to Willie, he's an all-year-rounder just like they are.'' She lowered her voice. ''If you make a fuss, you'll get Willie into trouble.''

''How?''

''If they think somebody knows about the lighter besides them, they won't be able to throw it in the lake to hide the evidence.''

I remembered how she had explained to me about fire-sale submarines the first day we met. She must know about this sort of thing, I thought.

''There you are,'' cawed Rose Bell. ''I was worried sick.'' She threw her wings around Sheila. ''What would I tell your mother?'' She took one step backward and slapped Sheila across the face. ''That's for scaring me half to death.'' They hugged each other.

''Where's Harley?'' asked Sheila.

''Safe in bed, no thanks to you,'' said Rose.

She looped her arm through Sheila's and began marching her toward the bungalows. Sheila never looked back.

I stood for a long time in a swirling crowd of firemen and policemen and women and children from the bungalow colony trying to figure out what to do next.

Then it hit me.

Harley set the fire.

I remembered standing with him on the meadow. He was gazing down at the softball field and the casino. He said: "I wish one of them would disappear. Then I wouldn't have to choose."

He had tried to make the casino disappear. Probably with wooden kitchen matches like the one I had slapped out of his hand that first time I had lunch with the group.

Harley had set the fire. He had left the rehearsal early and on his way out dropped a couple of lit matches behind the stage or in the kitchen or on some kerosene-soaked rags in the crawl space under the casino. The dry old boards of that firetrap must have gone up like a torch.

I elbowed out of the crowd and ran to the road. I almost got hit by a state police car. In the darkness I tripped in the ruts of the unpaved road, but I didn't stop running until Moe Bell shone his flashlight in my eyes and clutched my arm.

"Where are you going?"

"To your house," I blurted. "Harley set the fire."

"Shhhh." He pushed his face close to mine. "It's his casino, he'll inherit it someday. Nobody was badly hurt. Why do you want to ruin his life?"

"What?"

"You heard me." He turned me around and began walking me back toward the casino. "He'll never live down a black mark like this."

"He's only ten years old. They won't do anything to him. He won't go to jail."

"Lower your voice. I know that. But what happens ten years from now when he wants to get into law school and they find this on his permanent record?" His fingers were digging into my arm. "Don't say anything to anybody. Leave it to me."

"What are you going to do?" I had to jog to keep up with him.

"Don't worry, I'll handle it. I'm going to get Harley professional help. After this, I know Irving'll let him go to a doctor. Okay, Bobby?"

"Well . . ."

"Don't you want to give the boy a chance?"

"I guess so."

"Good. Now you just . . . what's going on here?"

A ghostly white balloon floated in a pool of dazzling light. It took a minute for my eyes to adjust. Willie Rumson's dopey moon face was caught in the cross fire of headlights from two police cars. He was grinning at the troopers who were handcuffing him. I thought I read his lips shape the words, "Sure, sure, sure," as they pushed him into the back of one of the cars.

"I've got to tell them," I said.

"Tell them what?" Moe tightened his grip on my arm.

"He couldn't have started the fire. He was down at the waterfront, dead drunk."

"Forget you saw him," said Moe. "He's trash, an animal. You want to take the responsibility of setting him free? To kill somebody next time?"

"He didn't do anything."

"You want to choose him over a little boy just starting out in life who still has a chance to straighten out and be a somebody?"

It was hard to think with Moe's face so close.

"Go home, Bobby. There's no camp tomorrow, I'm canceling, so all you've got to do is stay home and keep your mouth shut."

All the way home, Michelle raved about Jerry Silver.

"He was so wonderful, Bobby, so cool. We all started screaming when we saw the flames, but he just clapped his hands for attention, as if he had rehearsed it for years, he clapped his hands and shouted, 'You must listen to your king!'"

Michelle began laughing and crying simultaneously. She clutched the wheel of the car.

"He made us all hold hands, he ran up and down the line making sure every child was squeezing the hand of the child ahead and behind and then he made everybody sing, 'Getting to Know You' and he led us right through all that billowing smoke, we were crying and gagging, we couldn't see the people we were holding, it

187

was horrible, but he just kept singing, and he got us out.''

She wiped her eyes with the back of her hand, and the car swerved and missed a guardrail by an inch.

"And then he ran right back in there just to make sure everyone was out. That's when he burned his hand. Bobby, I'll never forget it as long as I live—it was the most wonderful . . .''

I said, "Michelle, I've got to tell you something. They arrested Willie Rumson . . .''

"I know. I was there when he wandered in and confessed.''

"He didn't do it. I know he was somewhere else at the time.''

She shrugged. "He's just an accident looking for a place to happen. He's better off behind bars before he kills somebody.''

Mom had gone to bed with a stack of teachers' manuals, but she got up to hear about the fire. I cut the cake and poured the milk while Michelle reenacted Silverstar's greatest performance. As soon as she was finished I said, "Harley set the fire and Willie Rumson's getting blamed for it.''

"Are you sure?" asked my mother. "Did you see Harley set the fire?"

"No, but Moe just about admitted it. And I know that Willie couldn't have done it because he was dead drunk at the waterfront."

"Have you told anyone yet?"

"Just Moe."

"What did he say?"

"To keep my mouth shut. Not to hurt Harley's chances of getting into law school. Can you imagine?"

My mother shrugged. "I can see his point. It would be awful if a man's future was ruined for a childhood prank."

"Prank?" I yelled. "You call that a prank? Your own daughter nearly got burned to a crisp . . ."

"Don't be so dramatic," said Michelle.

"Listen to her. And an innocent man is going to jail for a crime he didn't . . ."

"I would hardly call Willie Rumson an innocent man," said my mother. "Frankly, I've never been entirely comfortable since he got out of jail."

Suddenly, I felt weak and tired. "I'm going to bed."

"Good idea. I know your father will want to take you driving as soon as he gets home tomorrow." She smiled. "It's only a week to your test."

"I almost care," I said.

I walked into my room and threw myself on the bed. Why should I worry about Willie Rumson? He's better off in jail.

Why should I be so hard on Harley? If I hadn't maneuvered him into starting on the team and starring in the play, maybe he never would have set the fire.

And if I didn't keep my mouth shut, I could be making things worse for both of them. Willie on the loose could become a murderer someday. And Harley with a black mark on his permanent record might end up a wino.

I turned over and something dug into my backside. I pulled my pad and pencil out of my back pocket. The pencil point was broken and the pages of the pad were stuck together with sweat. As if it mattered.

In June I'd been so sure I'd fill a dozen notebooks with stories about racing fast cars on Drag Alley and going all the way with fast women on Make-Out Island and punching my way out of country bars while my buddies guarded my back. And the hand that wrote those stories was going to be as dark and hard as a mahogany knob.

So look at me now, no license yet, not a single new muscle, still a virgin.

Maybe I'll get something out of this summer after all. Maybe I'll finally learn to keep my big mouth shut.

Because if I don't, it's going to be a mess. I'll have to go to the police and tell them a story they don't want to hear and sign a statement and maybe take a lie detector test. I'd seen that in the movies but I couldn't figure out whether all those needles were taped to your skin or actually stuck into your body.

I hated needles.

20

Dad came home full of pep. "Boy, it's great to be out of that city. When's lunch, Lenore?"

"There's time for a swim if you want to."

"That means there's time for a drive." He tossed me the keys. "Today's the day, Robert. The county road."

"I just woke up. And I've got to talk to you. It's important."

"I'm sure it'll keep till this afternoon. Wash your face and button your pants. I want to get you on the road before the weekend traffic builds up."

The car started immediately. So far so good. I checked the rearview mirror, the side-view mirror, stuck my head out the window for landing planes, released the parking brake, checked the mirrors again, stepped on the clutch, shifted gears, rechecked the mirrors one more time, released the clutch, pressed the accelerator, and drove right into the garage door.

"I'm sorry." I couldn't help the whine in my voice. "I'm really sorry. I'll pay for it. I will. Out of my salary."

My father was laughing. "I'm glad we got that out of the way."

"What?"

"Your first accident. You can't learn to drive until you've had your first accident. It clears the air. Now you've had it. Welcome to the club. Take me to Lenape Falls."

I couldn't believe it. But I backed smoothly out of the driveway, guided the car slowly down the hill and made a neat, tight turn onto the county road.

"Perfect control," said my father. "Once we're past the lake take 'er up to forty."

"Forty miles an hour?"

"Relax and enjoy it."

After a while, I did. It was a beautiful ride. From the north end of Rumson Lake to the outskirts of Lenape Falls the road was ten miles of smooth blacktop that wound over rolling farmland and cut through a tall, dark woods and narrowed into a clattery one-lane bridge that spanned the muddy old Lenape River.

We opened the windows to let the cooling air rush in and to smell the rich, sweet aromas of August. Once I glanced at my father. He was smiling at me.

I don't think I made a single mistake. I shifted smoothly, I even passed a few cars. I felt wonderful. It wasn't until we were coming back, until we passed the sign that read: RUMSON LAKE—2 Miles, that I thought of Happy Valley and Willie and Harley, and felt the cold hard ball in my stomach.

"Dad? Remember that discussion we had about lying? If it's ever justified."

"Not that again." But his voice was light, almost jovial.

"Well, what about a situation where you keep your mouth shut. Is that a lie because you're not telling the truth?"

"Robert, as far as I'm concerned, there's true and there's false. No special situations. No summer rules. Case closed."

I waited until I saw our hill. "But if you don't tell it, it's not a lie, right?"

"We had a very successful ride. Let's not spoil it."

"It's important, Dad."

"Now, look." His voice wasn't light anymore. "I suppose this has something to do with the fire last night. You're trying to keep me talking until I say what you want to hear."

"No, I'm not . . ."

"Robert, if you're going to tell a lie, go tell a lie. If you're going to tell the truth, go tell the truth. But don't try to convince yourself that you're doing one thing when you're really doing the other. Then you'll be lying to yourself, too."

The ball in my stomach melted, but the sweat turned icy in my armpits and my tongue went dry.

"Robert, slow down. . . . Where are you going? . . . You'll miss the turn. Robert, you just passed the hill, what are you . . ."

"I'm driving to town, Dad. To the police station. Would you come inside with me?"

21

I didn't see Sheila or Harley again. I heard that Irving drove up to Happy Valley in the middle of the night, packed them into his Lincoln Continental, and drove right back to the city. The police wanted to talk to Harley, but they didn't make a federal case out of it. What were they going to do with him anyway?

Going to the police wasn't such a big deal. In fact, it was boring. I told my story to Sergeant Homer Smith, who had me repeat it to the Chief, who had me tell it again to some lawyers while a stenographer wrote it down. They thanked me, and when I asked them what would happen next, one of the lawyers said, in a polite way, that it was none of my business.

No needles.

A few days later, Jim Smith came by to tell me that Willie was upstate with one of his married brothers. Jim didn't get corny or even thank me too much, but he offered me a job until Labor Day, that same job I had been looking forward to back in June. He spent the rest of the afternoon fixing our garage door.

Dad called from the city that night and I asked him if I could take the job. He said, No, that it would look as though I was accepting a payoff for setting Willie free. I asked him if he still thought that the Smiths and the Rumsons were more dangerous than the characters at Happy Valley, and he said, "Robert, there's no time for philosophical discussions at long-distance phone rates. Good-bye." He hung up.

After Moe fired me, Michelle quit in protest. I was surprised and proud. So were Mom and Dad. Especially since Michelle quit before she found out that Moe was going to cancel the show. He said he was doing it for financial reasons, that he'd have to rent another casino for the production, but I was sure it was spite, the same reason he forfeited the softball games. If Harley couldn't play, nobody could play.

I never understood why Jerry and Al stayed on, and I never got the chance to ask them. In town, they would cross the street to avoid me. I'd say they were just gutless Bell henchmen, but how could you call Jerry gutless?

Michelle and I never got paid. Even at the seventy-five dollar utility counselor rate, Moe owed me $56.25. He told people that he didn't have to pay us because we were in breach of contract—we had both lied about our ages. I guess he always knew, even about Michelle.

But the summer wasn't a total loss financially. I got a ten-dollar tip from the mother of Steven, the Rumson Ranger I left alone because he was so well adjusted he didn't need the benefit of my psychological genius. In the letter she sent with the money, she thanked me for "helping Steven over his problem." She didn't mention what the problem had been.

I planned to spend the ten dollars on pencils, pads, and gasoline.